THE PERFECT AMERICAN

by

PETER STEPHAN JUNGK

translated by

MICHAEL HOFMANN

HANDSEL BOOKS

an imprint of
Other Press • New York

Originally published as *Der König von Amerika* by Peter Stephan Jungk

Klett-Cotta
Copyright © 2001 J.G. Cotta'sche Buchhandlung Nachfolger GmbH, Stuttgart

Translation copyright © 2004 Michael Hofmann

Production Editor: Robert D. Hack

This book was set in 11 point Janson by Alpha Graphics of Pittsfield, NH.

10 9 8 7 6 5 4 3 2 1

Library of Congress Cataloging-in-Publication Data

Jungk, Peter Stephan, 1952-
    [König von Amerika. English]
    The perfect American / by Peter Stephan Jungk ; translated by Michael Hofmann.
        p. cm.
    ISBN 1-59051-115-8 (alk. paper)
    1. Disney, Walt, 1901–1966–Fiction.   2. Dantine, Wilhelm–Fiction.
I. Hofmann, Michael, 1957 Aug. 25-   II. Title.
    PT2670.U53K6613 2003
    833'.914–dc22

                                                                2003024310

FOR ADAH

"My greatest creation is Walt Disney."
—Walt Disney

"When in doubt, tell the truth."
—Mark Twain

CHAPTER ONE

All is quiet.

He's been awake for half an hour. Awake and motionless. Lying on his back, ramrod-straight. The sun won't rise for a while yet. In the room next door, on the left, are Roy and Edna. His brother has never had trouble sleeping. Ever since his bout of TB in 1920, Roy has kept to a strict daily rhythm. He goes to bed before midnight. He gets up at seven. That's still two hours away.

Walt hasn't brought any reading matter with him, except for an issue of *Life* magazine, but that's on Lillian's side. He doesn't want to reach across or switch on a light, for fear of waking his wife. Both the television and the little transistor radio remain firmly off. He hears the wail of a train, six, seven, eight times in succession, a passenger train or a freight train that won't stop in Marceline. The hammering and drumming of wheels on the tracks goes quieter slowly, and becomes inaudible.

For four decades, I've gone from success to success, he whispers to himself, just as he does every morning in the moments between waking and getting up. There have been some setbacks, no doubt about that. But they were rare. Very rare. There were times when it looked as though we'd have to fire the entire workforce. Break up the studio. But Roy always

managed to talk them round, whoever they were, the bankers, the back-
ers, the shareholders. Roy, his elder brother by seven and a half years.
The realist in the family, who dreaded every change—more, tried to
prevent it from happening. Who never believed his youngest brother's
ideas could make money. Never mind: but for Roy, thinks Walt, our
enterprise wouldn't exist. The Bank of America must have advanced him
millions, over time. Walt doesn't quite understand how Roy did it. On
the other hand, he is perfectly aware that it is his, Walt's, imagination
alone that made possible the endless stream of credit. I was the first, he
says to himself, to give a distinct personality to cartoon films. I was the
first to work in color. The first to succeed in fitting sound tracks to trick
films. The first to produce a full-length animation feature. The first to
succeed in setting up a theme park that was neither squalid nor dirty nor
ugly. A little paradise on earth, my Anaheim empire. Walt takes immense
pleasure in having his past triumphs and present masterstrokes pass in
review: thirty-one, or is it thirty-two gilded Oscar statuettes I have been
awarded to date, more than anyone has before me, more than anyone else
will, ever. And six hundred and thirteen other miscellaneous awards,
distinctions, honorary doctorates, prizes, and medals from all over the
world.

I have so much to be grateful for, he says to himself every morning:
no matter how many times they try to kick me around, like a weeble I'll
wobble but I won't fall down.

It's only in the last few years, thinks Walt in the silence, that we've
finally been able to pay off our mountain of debt. It's only now that
every cent we make goes to us. Our company, our shareholders. And not
the bank. Only since my Anaheim empire. Only since my *Twenty Thousand Leagues Under the Sea* and the five episodes of *Davy Crockett* and the
101 Dalmatians and my *Mary Poppins*. After *Snow White* we did all right,
thirty years ago now. We were rich, Roy and I, for three, four, five years,
our wives could buy themselves whatever they liked. I took up polo—
before long, I had a dozen horses! The fat years, from '37 to '40! But then

followed *Pinocchio* and *Fantasia* and *Bambi*—and it seemed the good times were over.

Lillian and Walt, man and wife for forty-one years, have not slept in the same bed for twenty-five years. It's only on their travels that they end up sharing a bed, sometimes sharing their warmth, lying side by side. Separate beds—one of the conditions his wife put to him, following the great studio strike of the early '40s. If he wanted to remain married to her, then he would have to spend the night in his own bed. He was too restless at night. Too many times he woke her up to bother her with his worries, his fears, his doubts concerning himself and the world. A further condition attached to the marriage was that he must agree to adopt a child. Their own daughter, Diane, was three. She wanted someone to play with. Reluctantly he signed the necessary papers. And so Sharon came into his life. During the first few years, he saw her so rarely that he sometimes asked his wife who that little girl was, running around in the garden with Diane?

*

First streaks of light touch the sky over Marceline. Gradually, the room's fittings acquire contours. The large wardrobe. The bedside tables. The tulip-patterned curtains. The large ceiling light, with its seven spidery arms, and thinnish lightbulb on the end of each one. Once again, the wail of a locomotive, at once shrill and dull, a curious combination, loud and gentle, and the throbbing of its hundred wheels on the rails going past Marceline, no, not really past it, right through the middle of it, on its way from Chicago to Kansas City, or from Kansas City to Chicago, the characteristic sound of the place. Every twenty or thirty minutes, it breaks the rural silence.

I am a leader, a pioneer, I am one of the great men of our time, the words seem to echo within Walt. Ever since *Snow White* in 1937, he speaks this prayer in praise of himself every morning as he lies awake before sunrise. More people in the world know my name than that of Jesus Christ. Billions have seen at least one of my films. It's something that never existed before me: an art form, an idea, a concept, that managed to address and move and delight the whole of mankind. I have created a universe. My fame will outlast the centuries.

But here in Marceline, he adds on this particular Saturday, September 10, 1966, they practically worship me. Four years, Walt murmurs into the half-dark room, we lived here. I was four and a half when we came, and nine when we left. I come back far too rarely, it's ten years since I was last here.

In the afternoon, he is to open the new swimming pool and surrounding park in his name. Rarely has Walt felt so proud, not even the year before last, when a school for fourteen hundred pupils in Pittsburgh adopted his name. On that occasion too, he came; with the city fathers in attendance he cut the ribbon, but he left right after the celebration.

He eases himself out of bed, careful still not to wake Lillian, and gropes his way to the bathroom in the dark. For months now, he knows he should have gone to see a doctor, but he's kept putting it off. His neck hurts. There's a pulling and cramping in his right leg that he can hardly bear. His whole back is in pain. He switches on the light, and turns on the hot tap in the large tub.

His injury, sustained in the course of a polo match almost thirty years ago, torments him more than ever. He fell off his horse going after a ball he was never going to get, and in a game his team was never going to win. Pointless, really, to make the effort. But Walt and his teammates, Spencer Tracy among them, fought on, until the moment of the accident. "Never say die!" was one of Walt's principles. Three vertebrae in his neck were affected. They never healed. A fashionable Hollywood chiropractor whose clients included stars, directors, and producers had persuaded Walt that he could get better without recourse to a body cast. No corset for his back and no plaster for his upper body. A grave miscalculation, whose consequences he has suffered ever since.

He stretches out in the hot bath. Keeps adding more water, turns the hot tap on and off with the toes on his left foot. He hasn't been able to have a massage for two days now. The pain in his vertebrae is especially bad. In his studio in Burbank, he usually stretches out every evening at half past seven or eight, in a little room next to his office. It is decorated with photographs and drawings, and documents from his life: he calls it his laughing room. And there he pours himself a glass of Scotch, and receives heat treatment. Has his back, his neck, his hips and legs massaged. While Hazel George, the studio nurse, kneads his body, he permits her, his masseuse for twenty-five years now, certain insights into his life. He doesn't have many secrets. The few he does have, though, he shares with Hazel George and no one else.

Her treatments generally brought him relief, though it was mostly short-lived. Lately, he still feels the nagging pain, even after a whole series of compressions and thorough physiotherapy.

Their hosts, Mr. and Mrs. Othic, are sitting in their sunny kitchen in a pleasant state of excitement when Walt and Roy appear for breakfast shortly after seven. They are proud, very proud even, to have the brothers staying with them. Their acquaintance, one could almost call it friendship, goes back to the year 1956, when Walt came to lend his name to Marceline's elementary school. Fifty years ago, there was a small hotel in Marceline, called Allen's, above Murray's clothes store, on the town's main street, Kansas Avenue, very close to the railway station. It was closed down in the mid-forties, once Marceline had lost its importance as a coal-mining town and little railway junction. In the mid-sixties, there was only the one new motel on the edge of town, the Lamplighter, a badly built and ugly construction with small and squalid rooms. And since, ten years before that, neither the Allen nor the awful Lamplighter had existed, Walt called the mayor to tell him he'd rather stay with someone than get a room in Macon or Moberly, the only bigger towns in the vicinity. One thing he had to have, though, was air-conditioning, he said. That made things rather easy for Eddie Strayhall: of the two thousand four hundred and eighty-eight inhabitants of Marceline, there was only one man who had air-conditioning, and that was Othic, the prosperous farmer and mink breeder, who had had a magnificent villa built for himself on the corner of Kansas Avenue and Bisbee Street, with four bedrooms and two bathrooms. A long structure of red brick, unlike any other building in Marceline, you would have situated it in the better-off suburbs of a midwestern city, not smack dab in the prairie.

The two parties had remained in contact ever since—two of the little Othics had already visited Los Angeles several times at Walt's invitation, touring Disneyland as his personal guests. He escorted them from one attraction to the next. At Christmas, the two boys and the Othics' youngest daughter received generous gifts from Mr. Disney. All three of them were allowed to call him Uncle Walt, no, they had to, he absolutely insisted on it.

With the exception of one or two insiders, no one knew what time Walt had arrived in Marceline, and where he was staying. But as early as seven in the morning, there was a crowd gathered round the Lamplighter. Then the news spread like wildfire, Walt—as he had been ten years ago—was staying at the Othics'.

After breakfast, he smokes his first Lucky Strike of the day, right down to its unfiltered end, so far that his yellow-brown fingertips can barely grip its pinched stub. Then he lights the next off it, and smokes that down to the bitter end, too. Walt and Roy are wearing thin, charcoal, handmade suits from the Klein & Hutchinson fashion house on Cañon Drive in Beverly Hills, with white shirts and ties, Walt's being pale blue, and Roy's yellow ocher. As ever, Walt has a white handkerchief in his top pocket—and the same gold tiepin he's been wearing for years. Even out here in the country, the brothers stick to their self-imposed dress code. One exception: they put on boots this morning, black suede cowboy boots.

Lillian and Edna are still sleeping when their husbands leave the house. The previous evening, they took strong sedatives that Lillian never travels without. Edna too has suffered from insomnia for several years now. The brothers think they will succeed in strolling unremarked to the corner of Missouri Street and Broadway, where the farmhouse stands that was once, more than half a century ago, home to their family: Elias, their hot-tempered, thin, lanky father, their mother Flora, her mouth twisted with pain and her eyes almost always sad, their then-two-year-old sister Ruth, and their considerably older brothers Herbert and Raymond, who ran away from home then, because they could no longer stand Elias's meanness and injustice and the repeated beatings he gave them. Walt and Roy hope to be able to visit the creek where they used to go fishing with the neighboring Taylor boys and Clem Flickinger, without anyone in the town noticing and following them. They want to be alone, able to relive their memories undisturbed. They are looking forward to their expedition into the past.

The morning air bears the scent of fresh earth, cool grass, and a distant whiff of cowdung. September 10, 1966 is a Saturday. All the children are off from school. No sooner have the brothers gone one block north, out of town, at a quarter past eight in the morning, than the group that had been waiting for them outside the Lamplighter, comes running up, along with more and more people from Marceline, who have joined the original group, armed with notebooks, diaries, letter pads, equipped with pencils, crayons, ballpoints, and fountain pens. They lay siege to Walt. "Hey!" "Hi." "Yeah!" "Uhh!" "Me." "Sir." Other than that the only sound is the scraping of Walt's writing hand. No one asks for Roy's signature. All cluster round Walt, exclusively round him, with the urgency and single-mindedness of a swarm of bees clustering round the queen.

He gives autographs, thirty or forty of them, perfectly willingly, but without the least smile. And everyone is amazed at the difference between his signature and those rounded letters that are so readily associated with his name. How unlike the signature that graces the film posters, the opening frames of the television shows, the millions of children's books and comics.

A sunny day in late summer, with little white fluffy clouds. It's going to be warm later on, in Marceline, Missouri. The sky is crisscrossed with little streaks of condensation from the passenger airliners traversing the continent. The smell now is of freshly mown hay, ripe apples and apricots. Walt and Roy move off again—in spite of the great crowd ringing them.

"To the house!" Walt whispers to his brother.

"No, the creek first!" beseeches Roy, just as softly.

"The house first!" Walt repeats.

And Roy follows his younger brother. Without another word.

They march off toward the edge of town. Walt is coughing. The smoker's cough that has tormented him for twenty years has become acute. He has to stop for a minute. The horrible rattle of those coughing fits! He fights for breath.

The accompanying army steadily grows. More and more of Marceline's inhabitants emerge from their houses, and swell the procession following the Disney brothers to the wellsprings of their childhood.

One of those trailing along, joining the pilgrimage, is me, Wilhelm Dantine. The night before, I had taken a room at the Lamplighter, on the assumption Walt would be coming here. I was surprised that no one except myself and an elderly man from St. Louis were staying at the motel. Then, at six thirty, when I was drinking my morning coffee and devouring a frosted doughnut in the gas station across the road, I learned that the Disney brothers had been staying with private hosts. I had assumed there must be a wide selection of hotels or inns in Marceline; it is after all his Rosebud, the place where Walt spent his most crucial childhood years. People would turn up from all over the world, I thought, to view this particular little town for themselves. And when I arrived late in the evening, in the orange gloaming, I understood that I was the first visitor for a long time to have made my way here on the quest for Walt's past. The Lamplighter was primarily run for truck drivers and traveling salesmen. For outside of Marceline, hardly anyone knew of Walt's profound association with this place of his childhood. The previous day, I'd made a stop at a coffee shop in the little town of Meadville, only twenty miles or so to the west. The place had windows stuck with colored pictures of the mouse and the duck. When I got up to pay the check, I was asked where I was headed. I pointed to Mickey, Minnie, Donald, and company. The manageress of the coffee shop, fifty, curlers in her hair, and her two young waitresses, looked at me blankly. "To Marceline!" I added. Then I understood that while the ladies might dearly love Walt's creations, they didn't know a thing about the life and times of their creator.

I had taken fully five days to get here from Los Angeles, in my 1961 Rambler. It's not the first time I've hooked up with Walt on his travels. From time to time I show up in places where he appears, whether it's for film premieres, openings of shopping centers, or the awarding of prizes anywhere in the country. Whenever I've managed to hear of such an occasion in time, I've made a point of being there. I have been to six now since December 18, 1959, the day I was dismissed. He hasn't once recognized me. Two or three times I caught a look from him that gave me the sense: He's on to me. He has some faint memory. But then his little gray eyes moved on. Or seemed to look right through me. And that was the closest we got to making contact. I had long been planning to visit Marceline, for ten years and more. I wanted to see the place with my own eyes, but never got around to it, not until this day of late summer, 1966. It goes without saying, my journeys of pursuit haven't done much for my marriage or my family life. My wife accused me of preferring to live under Walt's continuing spell, instead of with her and our two sons.

The last time I had a close-up view of him was two years ago, at the San Diego Zoo. It was in the summer of 1964, and he was donating a lion cub that the visiting South African Prime Minister Hendrik Verwoerd had brought him as a gift. Walt seemed years younger, or that was my impression anyway. Now, in Marceline, he looked surprisingly aged, and also appeared rather less statesmanlike than he had on previous occasions when I'd been on hand to observe him. Perhaps it was that he felt he needed to disguise himself less, because he was more relaxed here in the heart of Missouri than anywhere else I'd seen him. Roy, on the other hand, whom I saw rather less often, seemed always the same, never changed. I thought he looked just exactly the way you'd picture an aging bookkeeper from the Midwest.

The brothers headed north up Missouri Avenue. Behind them was their army of escorts, by now they must have been around sixty strong. We kept—and, as I was right in their midst, I can vouch for this—a respectful distance. Not that our presence appeared to bother Walt and Roy all that much. They would turn around every few steps to look at us, but on neither of them did I detect any sign of animosity or annoyance. They were quite reconciled to making their personal pilgrimage in considerable company.

"Hey, you guys, my grandmother, Mrs. Passig, was your neighbor, do you remember her?" a young man called out. "She says Roy had a real crush on her. Is that true?"

"Hello, boys, remember me? Remember Eileen?" a robust, elderly woman cried out. She was wearing her Sunday best, a long black dress and a pert little pink hat. "Your mother used to buy thread from us. And almost everything you wore. I remember you as if it were yesterday, you two snotnoses."

Everybody laughed. On the corner of Missouri Avenue and Bigger Street, a new confluence of people joined our throng. Hurried along to the front, to be able to see the brothers from close up, but didn't dare ask for their autographs. One of the newcomers wore a broad, sand-colored cowboy hat, and a sheriff's badge on his washed-out denim shirt. He was unarmed.

"You're not from here, are you?" asked a twelve- or thirteen-year-old boy, who was walking along beside me. He had a fishing rod in his right hand.

"I moved here last month."

"I've never seen you before."

From early in the morning, I had taken care not to attract attention, not to be identified as being from out of town. Tucked my long hair under a Boston Red Sox baseball cap. Wore my plainest clothes—black jeans and a gray, shortsleeved shirt. My shoes, too, could hardly be any more worn, a scuffed pair of brown moccasins.

A few steps further, I was addressed by the elderly woman who had made everyone laugh a moment ago. "Hey there, hi, you're not from here, are you? I'm Eileen Murray. And who are you?" She seemed like a retired school principal.

I gave her the first name I happened to think of: "Charles."

"Charlie! Like Chaplin! And what else?"

"Webster. Charles Webster." That was a classmate of mine from high school, whom I never especially liked, and whose name I always gave when I didn't feel like giving my own.

"Pleased to meet you. Listen here, everyone, I want to introduce you all to Charlie Webster. And where are you from, if I may ask?"

"Originally from . . . New York."

"Is that a fact! We don't often get anyone coming here from quite that far away. And you've come on account of Walt?"

"Just passing through."

"That's most unusual. People don't come through here by chance. With us being so far from all the main routes."

The attention that was suddenly being paid to me was very disagreeable.

"Well, you've come on a very special day now, haven't you?" Mrs. Murray went on. "You've come on the day the swimming pool is being inaugurated. Congratulations!"

I nodded politely.

She herself, she continued, had been just eighteen when Walt's parents had moved down to Marceline from Chicago. "It's impossible to imagine it today, Mr. Webster, the way some people used to live out here, the conditions the Disneys had to endure. So poor! So basic! No electricity, of course, and you had to fetch the water from the well. No indoor toilet. Everything done outdoors, naturally, even in the middle of winter. In the deep snow. If you were very lucky, you had a little wooden outhouse, of the sort you find in Walt's early films a lot. America was like Africa is today. Our children and grandchildren don't think about that, of course, no one thinks about how things used to be, the way it really was out here. In the big cities, things were different, of course, more modern and so on. And then we had the Depression years, the twenties and thirties. Unimaginable, mister. I wonder, how old are you?"

"Almost thirty."

"Well, then of course you can't have any idea of how things once were, plus you're a city boy. My God, New York! You've got to picture it, the houses were full of fleas and all sorts of other vermin. Cockroaches, mice, rats. Before Walt's older brothers ran away from Marceline, Herbert, I mean, the dishonest one, and Raymond, the ugly one, seven people were living there together practically on top of each other. The five children shared one little room, even though the oldest were already fully grown. Incredibly nasty boys, both of them . . ."

"In what way?"

"They were rude, dissatisfied, quarrelsome, thuggish."

"What about Walt?"

"Delightful. Helpful. Amusing. Do you know what his favorite dish was?"

"No idea," I said, although I knew the answer, of course.

"His favorite dish was the apple pie his mother used to bake. Everyone in town loved Flora's apple pie. She made it with the apples she grew in her own garden."

I didn't need to ask Mrs. Murray twice to open her treasure chest of memories. It made her happy to share with me everything she knew about Walt's childhood. "He was terribly gifted. Even when he was only seven or eight, he was such a good artist! When he got back from school, and there wasn't anything he had to do to help his parents either in the house or on the farm, then he would lie out under the elm tree, you'll see it in a minute. He used to spend hours lying there, drawing whatever creatures ran or flew or hopped past, the chickens and ducks, crickets, ants, squirrels, crows and rabbits, deer, possums, mice. Mice, of course ... my God, the mice!"

Up ahead, Walt and Roy were walking faster and faster now, attempting to shake off their pursuers and companions after all. They did not succeed. And by the time the little crowd got to the corner of Missouri Street and Broadway, there were about a hundred of us, men, women, and children.

"That's the house!" Eileen Murray pointed at a two-story wooden house, painted dark red, which the Disney brothers were now walking up to. How many times Walt had used to tell us about the farm in Marceline! How many times he talked about moving from Chicago to Marceline. His father, an out-of-work carpenter, couldn't stand the city any more. Above all, the working-class district where the family was living in the northwest of Chicago, was becoming overrun by pimps and prostitutes. Elias Disney was afraid his two older sons, aged fifteen and seventeen, might go bad, if he didn't get them out of Chicago, and take the family out into the country. Elias's uncle, Robert, and his wife Margaret had bought a farm in Marceline a few years before, and the nephew now followed them out there, with wife and kids, and became a farmer.

Walt strode across the porch of his former home. He knocked on the front door. The current occupants showed him in: father, mother, and two overweight daughters. Eileen told me that the Westfalls had come from the nearby hamlet of New Cambria, and had bought up the former Disney farm, which was in a pretty ruinous condition a few years ago, along with some acres of land, and had just begun cultivating it again. I watched as Walt showed the Westfalls the place on the southern wall of the building where as an eight-year-old, he had drawn a pig with tar, twelve feet long and eight feet high. He had drawn it one market day, when his parents had gone to Macon to buy a sow.

"In the evening, when Father and Mother got back," it was the first time in two years that I got to hear his soft, deep, and melodious voice, and, as it always did, it sent a shiver down my spine, "and saw my work of art, and the fact that half the wall was smeared full of tar, I knew I was in for a hiding. I got it from my father across the backside. And a couple of slaps from my mother."

The brothers were invited into the house to take a look at the rooms they had once lived in. A short, sixty-year-old man appeared between them, and gave Walt a powerful hug. Clem Flickinger, as Mrs. Murray went on to tell me, was a neighbor from those days, and Walt's best friend, with whom he played every day. His other friends, the Taylor boys, John and Fred, had moved away long ago. Walt's youngest sister Ruth, who at the age of three had fallen in love with the eight-year-old John Taylor, had gone back to Marceline in 1950, to look for her old flame. But he wasn't living here any more, they said he was killed on June 6, 1944, one of the first to die in the Normandy invasion.

"It was Clem who showed Walt how to trap fish with his bare hands," Eileen whispered to me. "The pair of them were both born in the same year, 1901, just a few months apart. Come along, I'll show you the tree, would you like that? While the boys are inside the house. . . . Did I say something wrong, Mr. Webster? They're still boys to me, nothing's changed." She led me another thirty yards or so further along Broadway, which was no wider than a trail at that point. There, in the middle of a pasture behind the house, was an ancient, mighty elm. I went up to it, stroked its rough, gray bark, pressed my hands against the trunk, reached up for leaves trembling in the wind.

"This is where he used to lie, right here, I can still see it so clearly in my mind's eye, he was lying on his stomach, with pencils and paper, some kind of rough brown packing paper, because no one around here could have afforded fine white paper, and he would lie there stretched out, and he would draw and draw and draw, my God, for hours and hours."

I had a little Kodak Instamatic on me, and I pulled it out, extended my arm, and took a picture of myself against part of the tree trunk that looked like the cogwheels of some great engine, as the bark was marked with ten longish circular seams, strangely regular in the way they were pressed together.

"Am I right in thinking you have some interest in Walt, then?" my companion suddenly wondered. "You could have asked me, if you'd wanted your picture taken under Walt's meditating tree, or his belly-button tree, as I always liked to call it, because he would lie on his belly button, and draw and paint. For heaven's sake, I could have taken that picture for you!"

I took a picture of her, she laughed, a little bashfully looking at the ground, called out, "Oh no, please, you mustn't!" but was nevertheless quite pleased.

Walt never told us about that tree.

I crushed a leaf between my fingers, and sniffed its bitter smell. Pulled off a leafy twig, and stashed it in my jacket pocket. I noticed that a spring bubbled up right next to the roots, that made a narrow stream flowing in the direction of the open fields.

Mrs. Murray could have had no idea how much her words electrified me, kept provoking my curiosity. Still, she obviously enjoyed having taken me, the only outsider, under her wing.

"Also the business with the owl, which almost no one knows about here, Mr. Webster," she continued. "Clem, I guess, would know the story. No one else, though. Do you want to hear it? Walt was lying out here one Sunday, same as always, thinking about life and drawing, and then he suddenly heard the call of an owl, directly above him, here in these branches. A brother of his father's, whom he liked very much, often came to stay, he didn't have a place of his own, he lived here and there, he vanished, came back another time. Walt called him his Uncle Elf, because he really was like a kind of good fairy to him, and Elf had always warned Walt about owls being messengers of death. Anyone who heard an owl cry outside his window was sure to die the next day. Walt leaped up before the owl could get away, grabbed it by its feet. Imagine how it must have cried, the poor creature, as he throttled and stamped it to death. The howling and hissing! It gave Walt goosepimples all down his back, on his neck and his scalp. And then he buried it, the poor little screech-owl, here, deep under this tree. I can show you the place, it's there, right next to the spring. . . . Strange, isn't it? Because owls are really among the deadliest enemies a mouse can have, owls and cats, right?"

Walt and Roy emerged from the house, accompanied by Clem Flickinger and the Westfall family. The little group seemed to make straight for the elm tree.

"Now, Mr. Webster, do you see where they've stopped, the boys, on that bit of open ground, there used to be a barn there, it was so pretty, and that's where Walt made his first money. He dressed the ducks and the rabbits and the little piglets in clothes, funny little wool pants and shirts. They looked real silly. Then he got people to come and look at them, and charged a few pennies' admission from everyone, including me, of course. I must have been the oldest member of his audience. Then, I read in the newspaper, a couple of years ago, he had the barn remade in Los Angeles, a perfect copy, from old photographs. A little piece of Marceline he always wanted to have with him."

I moved on, until I found myself again in the crowd of onlookers, who had reached the pasture by now.

"Ah, the stranger—still with us?" called the boy with the fishing rod, whom I had avoided earlier. He waved, pleased to see me.

"Michael, my grandson," Mrs. Murray presented him, "a sweet, bright, little fellow. Walt at the same age must have been just like him . . ."

"Gran, the gentleman says he's been living in Marceline for a month. That's not right, is it? We would have known, wouldn't we?"

Mrs. Murray smiled. "We're a very close-knit community, here in Marceline. There are no blacks here, no Asians, no descendants from any

Indian tribes, thank God. We can tell right away if someone belongs or not. Anyone wearing a Red Sox cap around here? Well, then!"

The boy was delighted. "It's like Reverend Brown always preaches, lies have short legs."

"A misunderstanding," I muttered.

Walt now clasped the thick trunk of the elm, embraced it, pressed his temple hard against the bark, so hard that his cheek got squashed upward and half-pressed his eye shut. In all the years I had known him, I had never seen him do anything as passionate. Then he let go, wiped his cheek, straightened his tie, brushed off the bits of bark that had stuck to his jacket, and plunged his hands into his trouser pockets.

"He's looking for a coin," whispered Mrs. Murray. "It's a superstition with us, dropping a coin in the spring for good fortune."

For a while he scrutinized the flat of his hand. And then exclaimed, loud enough for everyone to hear: "Not a single penny. Nothing but silver, nickels and dimes and quarters!" And the money jingled back into his pocket.

Walt opened his arms, took in the fields on either side of the property. "Down there by the pond," he said, "that was the place where I always used to ride on Porker, the great sow. She always let me up, no problem, and I used to ride what, twenty, thirty yards. Until the point, always the same point just by the mudhole, where she used to throw me! That pig was my favorite animal, and I'm quite certain she understood every word I said to her. She was incredibly clever. I persuaded Dad not to have her butchered. We played that game all the time I lived here: getting on her back, riding, being thrown . . . It was the most fun I ever had."

"Of course, when he was a boy, he saw all the usual country things," Eileen resumed. "Slaughtering and butchering, reaping and sowing, the birth and death of cows and horses, cats and dogs. There was only one time he was present when a pig was slaughtered—and he was so disgusted.

They say he's never been able to stand the sight of blood since, neither animal nor human blood. When I was little, I always thought it was exciting somehow, animals being slaughtered. Watching a butchered pig or calf or goat being hung upside down and bled on a hook. But I was more like a boy in that way. And Walt was more like a girl. He couldn't stand it. Watching the intestines spilling out. He couldn't take the smell either."

"Here," I heard Roy whisper to his brother. I still had very keen hearing then. "This is where we watched the rabbits, you know! Were they ever wild and energetic!"

"And here," Walt pointed the other way, "is where we caught that damned fox who used to steal our chickens . . ."

". . . and that I wasn't allowed to kill, because you were so sensitive!"

All at once, he started walking straight toward me; my knees turned to jelly. For perhaps half a second, Walt Disney looked me straight in the eye. And walked past, without once turning back.

"And there's the pond," he threw his arm around Clem, "where at break of day we would sit on the bank and imitate the call of ducks. And got all the drakes for miles around to come here! The fury and the disappointment when they realized they'd been tricked, real temper tantrums . . ." He mimicked the call, the female's plaintive gurgling that I'd heard so often from him in the past. It still sounded utterly convincing.

*

When the crowd reached the narrow creek on the end of Julip Road, a quarter of a mile from the center of town, I counted two hundred people. All in commotion. All in uproar. Like the anthill where you dropped twigs or matchsticks as a child, to watch the wild panic and bustle of the tiny creatures.

We stood pressed tight on a bridge. The Disney brothers pulled off their jackets and rolled up their sleeves, and reached into the murky waters of the Wolf River with their bare hands, encouraged and advised by Clem.

They caught nothing.

Michael, though, had cast his line from the bridge, and after a few minutes had hooked a decent-sized catfish. Now he carried the twitching, dying creature down the bank, to offer it as a present to Walt and Roy. Cheers and applause rang out from all sides, paying tribute to Marceline's favorite sons. Walt looked aside as, with Roy's help, the boy laid the fish on a flat stone. Bashed and bashed a rock on its bony head, until it was dead.

"Was that a deer in the bushes behind me? Or was I imagining things?"

"Here, on the Wolf River?" Eileen laughed at me. Not for thinking I might have spotted a deer, but for doubting the fact. "My Lord. There's any number of them. They've become quite a nuisance. But at least it's the hunting season soon!"

We all accompanied the guests of honor to the Sherwood family residence on the corner of Chestnut and California. Here the brothers were expected for lunch. It was only ten a.m. The door opened. They were welcomed, two hours early. This was the farm of Doc Sherwood's descendants. His maize and millet fields were the largest in Marceline at the beginning of the century. He had more livestock than anyone else in town. Trained in Chicago, he was the only doctor for many miles around. He had an old plough horse, Old Man, and Walt is said to have spent a lot of time watching the animal when it was so tired it could barely set one foot before another. He made a sketch of it when he was eight. The drawing of the exhausted horse, in soft and hard pencil, pleased Doc Sherwood so much that he paid the boy what was at the time—the summer of 1909—a small fortune: twenty-five cents.

Walt turned to face the crowd. "We'll see you all in the afternoon!" he called out. "Thank you for the friendly escort!" Waved and disappeared with Roy into the modest farmhouse, pleased to be away from the horde for a couple of hours. A murmur went through the mass, people had counted on spending the whole day in the company of the Disneys. One or two individuals even knocked on the Sherwoods' door, and some, the sheriff among them, looked in through the windows. No one was admitted, not even Clem, not Michael, whose catch Roy had wrapped in a sheet of newspaper and taken into the house.

Slowly, tactfully, people left the scene. Only some of the children remained in the vicinity of the farm, either propped against tree trunks, old trailers, fresh haystacks, or else sitting in the cut grass. It had gotten very hot by now.

"Why don't you come over," Mrs. Murray took my hand in hers, "I'll make you lunch and we'll get acquainted a little."

"Thank you, ma'am." I took my hand away, excused myself, said I didn't want to disappoint her, but I preferred to be on my own for a while.

First, I passed the coal chute, which hadn't been in use for decades, a ruined, rusty metal structure that soared into the sky. This was where the locomotives from the Atchison, Topeka & Santa Fe Line used to stop to take on coal, across two pairs of rails. The station was next, an empty, two-story brick building, only the dirty little waiting room was still intact, and that smelled of cigarette smoke, pee, and moldering wood. The windows were all broken, shards of glass lay scattered on the cracked platform. On the weathered station sign, the letters L and N were missing. An express train sped through the station, with a rush of air and a howling cry. The splendid diesel locomotive bore the name *Santa Fe Super Chief* on it in big red letters, and I counted the cars, like I did as a child when we had moved to Los Angeles and were living in Encino, which was right next to the lines. I tried, as I did then, to see individual passengers, but could only make out the white-hatted chef, who was standing motionless by the kitchen window of the dining car, smoking a cigarette and staring out at the view.

Five minutes later, a local train stopped, coming from Quincy, Illinois, bound for Kansas City. No one got out. No one got on.

There was a little park beside the station, named after E. P. Ripley, the longtime president of the Santa Fe Railway company, later to become a close friend of Walt and Roy. In the middle of it was a small pavillion, where open-air concerts were held on Sundays and holidays, and at one end of it an old steam locomotive from the thirties, that the children of Marceline liked to climb all over and play in. On the other side of the lawn Kansas Avenue began, the town's main street, bordered on either side by typical, low, small-town buildings. A banner had been put up across the street, and was fluttering now in the warm breeze. "Welcome Back Walt and Roy," it read.

Marceline's fire station, barber's shop, town hall, candy shop, and clothes store, even the little movie house: they all strikingly resembled the buildings along Main Street U.S.A., the principal artery in Disneyland. The closest resemblance was in the case of the corner building that had once housed the Hotel Allen, but was now empty, and slowly, slowly crumbling away. The same colors and materials and window casements, the same roof shape all occur in the physical reincarnation of Walt's fantasy world—only a tad smaller than in the original. In the course of an argument once, he had openly admitted to me that his Anaheim empire was based on the layout of Marceline. Not until September 10, 1966 did I see for myself how much truth there was in that confession. The railway line that went around the Magic Kingdom, and Walt's whole obsession with steam locomotives, stations, rails, level crossings, passenger cars, and dining cars, could be traced back to this little town in Missouri, where the trains passed through.

Eileen's older son Edgar ran Murray's clothes store, which had been in the family ever since 1898. It was on the ground floor of Allen's. Here, Flora Disney had bought Walt his first overalls in 1906. When I walked into the store, sixty years later, I marveled at the mahogany-framed glass cases that had stood there since the beginning of the century. Edgar, a fellow with a pasty face, red cheeks, and tiny eyes, had been called by his mother just before I came in. "Yes, Mom, I promise," I heard him say, two or even three times. As he put the receiver down, I was already standing next to him.

Patiently he led me round the whole of the dark, ballroom-sized space, showed me all the stock, including probably the oddest collection of ladies' hats I ever saw.

"What brings you to us, Mr. Webster?" he asked me then.

"I just happened to be passing through."

"But didn't you tell my son Michael you'd been living here for a month already?"

"That was . . . a mistake."

"Mistake?"

"A . . . misunderstanding."

"And what is it that you do professionally, if I might ask?"

"I help in my dad's business. He's not doing too well right now, health-wise."

"I thought you came from New York? I saw your Rambler outside the Lamplighter. Your plates are from Chicago. Why is that?"

"Because . . . I was coming from Los Angeles, I mean to say Chicago . . . because my father lives there."

"America's a free country, Mr. Webster. You can come and go as you please. I was only wondering . . ."

"My father owns a chain of dry-cleaners. A couple of years ago, he asked me to scout around to see whether there was a chance of expanding into some other states."

"Sure, why wouldn't there be?"

"Right . . ."

"But what is it that brings you to Marceline, of all places?"

"As I was saying, we were thinking . . . of trying to move into Missouri . . ."

"So that's why you're living in New York . . . just now."

"I get around a lot."

"Do you like it here?"

"Very much. It's a nice place."

"It's Walt's place."

"So I saw today."

"The best is still to come, Mr. Webster—the official inauguration of the swimming pool and our new town park. How odd that you should be here at the same time as Walt and Roy . . ."

"Just lucky, I guess." I bought a pair of gray socks off Edgar Murray for a dollar—seventy-five percent polyester, twenty-five percent cotton—and started for the door.

"In the Lamplighter, they said they didn't have anyone staying under the name of Webster."

I broke out in a sweat. "When I'm on the road I often use my mother's maiden name."

"Sure you do." And, after a pause. "And why is that?"

*

As I walked off, I wondered if it wouldn't be more sensible to break off my stay in Marceline. But the persistent desire to see Walt again, hear his voice, observe his movements, even if for just a couple of minutes, prevailed. And the possibility I might finally be able to carry out my plan that night seemed almost tangibly within reach. I trembled. How would the encounter go? When would it take place? I desperately needed to rest before the opening ceremony. I'd spent most of the night lying awake.

After the gray brown concrete structure of the Bethany Baptist Church on Howell Street, which stretched out for an entire block to Santa Fe Street, came the Walt Disney Elementary School. I remembered Walt's accounts of his 1956 trip back to Missouri. There had been a little scene during the official opening ceremony. Walt got up before the invited dignitaries, and opened with the sentence: "I have slept with two of the women present in this hall." Lillian was seated at the head table, next to her husband. The smile froze on her lips. A gasp of horror went through the hall, on his own account. A few parents got up to leave. Then Walt added: "The other one is my former babysitter, Miss Lola Harrity, who's sitting in the front row." The audience sighed with relief, a few managed to chortle. "Miss Harrity, who always used to smell so wonderful," Walt went on, "would have to slip into bed with me when my parents and my brothers were still getting in the harvest late at night, or otherwise out somewhere. She looked after me and my sister Ruth, and we paid her in butter and milk. I cried every time she came, claimed I couldn't possibly sleep unless she was lying next to me." Miss Harrity had turned beet red, looked strickenly at the floor. Soon afterward, apparently, she died, a little short of seventy.

"Are you looking to go in there?" It was Michael's voice behind me. He must have come after me, and I hadn't noticed. "The gate's always left unlocked." He showed me to a large glass-fronted cabinet near the front door. There was a wooden school bench with wrought iron legs. On the gently sloping top, I saw the letters *WD*, carved with a penknife in a couple of places. My initials, Walt's initials. "Guess who that bench might have belonged to, Mr. Webster! You've got it, haven't you? Because Park School, which Walt attended, was on the same site as this school. Grandmother says he was a good pupil, not like me. He could read and write quite well, says Granny, that's what they taught him here in Marceline! I only like to hunt and fish, so I don't really care that I'm not such a good pupil."

Not without pride, he showed me the school assembly hall and gymnasium, decorated by Walt's publicity man Bob Moore with outsize Disney figures. I thought my senses were playing a trick on me. Weren't those the very first figures I ever drew for Walt, in late 1955? The two chipmunks, Chip 'n' Dale, the way they appeared in the Donald Duck film *Chips Ahoy*, which meant that they were definitely in *my* version, and not in the rather dissimilar ones by Ollie Johnston or Ham Luske or Milt Kahl. No, only I drew that way, no one else. Evidently, no one had considered it worthwhile asking me for my permission. Neither Walt nor Bob Moore had troubled to find out whether I had any objection to my Chip and my Dale hanging on the gym wall of some elementary school in the Midwest. They didn't breathe a word to me, not even after they got back.

I stood in the empty gym, staring at the flaking beige walls. Suddenly, I felt dizzy, I had to sit down. Michael pushed up a sky-blue stool.

"Are you hungry, Mister?" he asked me. "Grandmother says you should definitely eat some lunch, I'm to tell you."

*

At the gas station next to the Lamplighter, I had them shove a pizza in the oven for me. You couldn't eat your food on the premises, and there was nowhere to sit down. The Mobil Oil employee put the pizza in a cardboard box, which I carried the few steps to the motel. Then I sat down at a narrow vanity table under a picture of Mickey and Minnie, turning their backs on the viewer and gazing into the sunset over Los Angeles, arm in arm. I wolfed down the cheese, salami, mushroom, and tomato mix that tasted of water, papier-mâché, and salt. Laid down then, fully clothed, on the soft, sagging double bed in the windowless Room 3, and fell into an uncommonly deep afternoon sleep.

A dream went with me. It wasn't the first time I had dreamed it. Twenty-four minutely distinguished Chip 'n' Dale drawings make up a second of animation film. Two hundred and forty drawings of chain-smoking earth-worms equal ten seconds of movement. One thousand four hundred and forty individual drawings of a dog family on skates, a baby rabbit at a piano, two chickens in a racing car, each one a tiny bit different from the one before, will make a minute of cartoon. In my dream, the shadows split off from the bodies, raging pirates burst asunder, octopuses turned into elephants. A little fish became a donkey. Locomotives ate cookies, auto-mobiles flirted with crocodiles, bees metamorphosed into bonbons, bonbons into airplanes. But in the airplanes sat *my* chipmunks, bombing a small town with hazelnuts. A five-minute film with the blue uniformed drake, who fell off a cliff and carried on calmly marching through the air, until he noticed what he was doing, whereupon he promptly plummeted, and then fell off a cliff again, only this time he put out his hand at the last moment for a branch, and went on falling and falling, as his arm grew longer and longer, twenty yards, like a thick elastic band, and, once at the bottom he shot back up, and so on and so forth. A short like that was put together from over seven thousand two hundred individual drawings. One hundred and thirty thousand finely painted color pictures made up the full-length feature film *Sleeping Beauty*, and fully one third of the original *Sleeping Beauty* sketches were by me, Wilhelm Dantine. And then the dream would begin all over again—numbers, figures, animals, shapes, shadows, and so on, the squeal of brakes, the laughter of chickens, the magic of three fairies, always in a ring, mingled with my longing for my profession to which I clung with every fiber of my being, which ended so abruptly in December 1959. What a magnificent profession it was: to make characters move beautifully, to make them live, breathe, and think.

I was awakened by the wailing of a locomotive. Looked at my watch. It was five o'clock. I take a nap after lunch almost every day, but never longer than fifteen or twenty minutes. Sleeping for three hours in the middle of the day, that certainly hadn't happened to me for many years.

I felt more exhausted than before my sleep. I got up. My footsteps led me back to the Sherwood farm. The sunlight seemed harsher, the scents of hay and apples and apricots stronger than they had in the morning. There was no one left around the farmhouse. I cautiously went up to one of the little windows and peeped inside. The table in the middle of the room was still laid, overflowing with plates, water jugs, bottles of fruit juice, and leftovers. I reckon ten people or so had sat down at it. On an old worn armchair there was a copy of the *Kansas City Star*. "South African Prime Minister Stabbed to Death in Pretoria Parliament," read the headline, which was all I could make out. How strange: the last time I'd seen Walt had been at the San Diego Zoo, when he'd presented them with the lion cub that was Hendrik Verwoerd's present to him.

It was the *Kansas City Star* that he'd delivered as a boy on his paper route, every morning before sunrise. This was after the family had left Marceline in the fall of 1910 and had moved to Kansas City. It was the same newspaper that he applied to later, at nineteen, for a job as a cartoonist. He was rejected. On the grounds that he was insufficiently gifted as a draftsman, and that his satirical vein was at best mediocre. He needed far more punch, they told him, some cynical insight into political events.

I walked back downtown. Murray's was closed, even the gas station was deserted. I passed nine churches on a very short stretch, all of them dark and shut, and with little signs on their doors: "Evening prayers canceled." I encountered no one. There was complete silence everywhere. Reached the edge of town again, the southern end of Kansas Avenue. Finally, I heard brass band music, laughter, children yelling. I headed for the noise. It was six o'clock.

All the inhabitants of Marceline had flowed out here, to this little park with its shallow pond. More than two thousand people were now making their way up the hill on whose crest the new swimming pool was situated. The sheriff was wearing a newly pressed, beige uniform—and a couple of revolvers on his belt. A dozen police officers had been recruited from Macon to make sure that the festive but extremely well-behaved crowd was kept in check. The onlookers formed up in a large tightly drawn semicircle around a wooden stage that looked to have been hastily thrown together near the entrance to the open-air pool. Right in front were the children of Marceline, either kneeling or sitting on the grass, behind them older kids, and behind them the grown-ups. All seemed to be following some unwritten rules.

Sellers of balloons and popcorn and Coke took up their places in the semicircle, quite as though they'd rehearsed this arrangement for the past several days. I went to where the children sat. "Hey!" came a cry from behind, "you go to the back!"

Time for a long look at the swimming pool; I had imagined an Olympic-size pool, a magnificent sports center like you might have in a city. But the pool of pale blue painted concrete was twenty feet wide and maybe fifty in length at the most. There wasn't any water in it yet, perhaps to prevent exuberant onlookers from taking a dip either before or immediately after the opening ceremony.

"C'mon!" more whistles and catcalls, "get away from the front!"

I looked to see if I could spot Mrs. Murray anywhere, I was quite keen not to have her pop up at my side just at that particular moment. Instead, Edgar hurried up to me, pulled me toward the back rows. He was standing with his mother and son some way from the wooden stage.

"Well finally," twittered Eileen; she had changed, and was now wearing a yellow chiffon dress with a large red paper rose on the lapel. Her large black straw hat would have looked more at home in Ascot than Marceline, Missouri. "We were afraid you'd left already, without saying good-bye to us. Edgar thought he'd made you angry, sort of. And Mike says you looked very pale and weak when he saw you at lunchtime today."

Just as I was about to reply, a huge and unanimous cheer went up. The only time I experienced anything like it was in the London Palladium in fall 1965, before and during a Beatles concert. The Othics' black Cadillac drew up at seven o'clock sharp, down on the oversized parking lot, which was two-thirds empty. Walt climbed out, followed by Lillian, the Othics, Roy, and Edna. It was the first time in all those years I had had a glimpse of Mrs. Disney from up close. She looked much more attractive than I had expected. I had imagined her as careworn and unappealing, but she was tall and rather distinguished-looking.

Walt climbed swiftly up on to the improvised podium. There was a surge of applause, which took a minute or so to die down. The fatigue he had felt from the demands of the morning seemed gone. He had recovered his beaming smile, and looked perfectly ageless. After the mayor had spoken a word or two of welcome, he stepped up to the microphone.

It took a further while before he could make himself heard. He began by pointing to the security cordon separating him from the crowd. "This is my home. I don't need police protection!"

Cheers, applause.

"My most precious memories," he went on, "as you know, have to do with my years in Marceline." He turned away from the microphone, trying to shake off a sudden fit of coughing. There was silence on the slope in the little park. At last, he was able to go on: "I'm sorry for people who have to spend their entire lives in big cities. People who aren't fortunate enough to be at home in a small community, as I was. You kids, growing up in Marceline, do you know how lucky you are? The most important things that ever happened to me, happened here—when I was a child here, I experienced more than I expect I'll live to see in the rest of my life." There was thunderous applause. He lapped it up, enjoyed every single handclap. "All the things that were to matter to me later were things I came across here. Not just country living, but my first circus and the circus parade that went marching down Kansas Avenue. And where did I see my first film, *The Life of Christ?* Well, in Marceline, on Main Street, of course, in the movie theater that's still standing today, sixty years later.... The unhappiest moment of my entire childhood was the day we moved away, in 1910. Oh, how I missed Marceline! The one good thing about Kansas City was that it was only ninety miles away from here. In 1923, I moved on from Kansas City to Los Angeles. As you can imagine, I traveled on the Santa Fe Super Chief. The Atchison, Topeka & Santa Fe Line tells the story of my life. It begins in Chicago, where I was born. The train stops in Springfield, Illinois, where my idol Abraham Lincoln is buried, and then a few hours on in Marceline, which was a little railway junction town. The next major station: Kansas City, where we lived for thirteen years. And the end of the line? Los Angeles, where I went when I was twenty-two. Even though I was almost penniless, I bought myself a first-class ticket—and the story of what happened to me then, out in Hollywood, well, some of you may've heard a bit about that already." Laughter welled up around him, and echoed on.

As he spoke, darkness slowly fell. A single searchlight dipped him in its harsh beam. He paused when a long freight train clattered by—the park was right next to the tracks. "Music to my ears; anyone who knows me at all will tell you, isn't that right?" he resumed, once things had quieted down. The evening cool came on. I was shivering, I should have put on a sweater after my nap. "So, you know what Roy and I have achieved in Hollywood. But you must understand, I don't just make films for kids, I make films for all ages and for all people. And what gives me the inner strength to do this? The source I draw on is here, in the heart of Missouri. The naturalness, the simple, direct, straightforward manner so typical of you, which I was privileged to encounter as a boy, shaped me, and I had to hand it on, and give it to the rest of humanity. Only someone who has seen and smelled and been touched by Marceline will be able to understand. I am Marceline, and everything I've become has its roots here."

He paused to catch his breath. This was my chance, I thought, my moment had finally come.

"You know I find it difficult to speak without notes. I'm not good at it," he went on, before I could begin to act. "I remained a farmer's boy, all my life. A country boy, hiding behind a mouse and a duck. Today, my wife, my brother, my sister-in-law, we were all guests of the Sherwood family—and it felt to me as though I were traveling in a time machine. I was eight years old again, I was sketching Doc's horse Old Man. The Sherwoods are like their forefathers, like their great-grandfather. They've remained true to their family tradition. You all have remained true to your family traditions. There is no crime in Marceline. There are no Negro riots here, no Vietnam War demonstrations, no burning of draft cards, no long-haired, drug-taking hippies, God forbid. No, here among you, among *us*, I dare say, there is peace, health, faith. This is the America I belong to. When I was with the Sherwoods, I asked to see my drawing from 1909, which they keep in a safe, and I offered them, or rather, as I have always steered clear of money matters, Roy offered them, ten thousand dollars in cash for that picture which I drew as a child, and for which Doc Sherwood once paid me a quarter." This time there was a kind of collective groan that went up from the assembled masses. "That's right, ten grand. Do you know what the Sherwood family's reply was? 'Even if you were to offer us a hundred thousand, or a million, we would never sell you that picture!' You see, that's what I admire about you all. You're proud and principled. Now, in gratitude for all that Marceline means to me, I made a decision this afternoon, while I was in the Othics' house, preparing myself for tonight: I want to base the Walt Disney Childhood Farm here in Marceline, right by the farm where we used to live. A place where kids will learn how to plant and sow and reap. A kind of model farm. To bake bread, to make butter, milk cows, and bottle milk. A place where we'll teach them how pigs and goats and geese and rabbits live and thrive, how they ... well, reproduce! In other words, from next spring, there's going to be a great building site here, because I'm convinced that the children of the future will have to be taught about life on a farm, just like today we teach them the three R's. Because the children of the future aren't going to know these kind of things anymore: What a seed grain looks like. The way you plant an apple tree. How you grow rye and make flour. The children of the future aren't going to know where milk and cheese come from. Where the eggs come from they eat for breakfast! Well, they'll be arriving from all over the country, and they'll be able to learn all those things right here, next to the farm on which I myself grew up."

He must have counted on joyful applause at this point. But there was silence, an eerie silence.

"That's right, next to the farm of my childhood ..." he sounded quieter, a little more hesitant. "But we can see about that ... next year ... or maybe the year after, I'll be back, and Roy too of course ... when the time comes. For today, ... it's my great pleasure to dedicate the new Marceline swimming ... the first public pool of the town of Marceline ... to declare ... I hereby pronounce ... say, have we got a champagne bottle? To smash against the side of the pool, the way they do when they launch ships? No? Too bad! Although ... well, I guess you'd have to ... sweep up the broken glass later ... Anyway: I hereby name the new sports center of my former hometown the Walt Disney Park."

In the confusion following Walt's speech, a mixture of applause, shouts, bits of talk, hollering, and running around, it would have been an easy matter to execute my plan. It would have been the perfect moment. The best and likeliest situation that was ever offered to me in all those years. Before the entire population of Marceline, in front of his wife, his brother, his sister-in-law, I just needed to dare.

I didn't.

"Mr. Webster!" I heard Mrs. Murray call out behind me. "Charlie!" yelled her grandson, but I ran through the dark, ran as fast as my legs would carry me. Reached the car that was parked outside the Lamplighter. And drove off, breathless for the first ten minutes, along Highway 36, headed for Kansas City.

I didn't stop until I was almost there, and then I studied the maps, and drew up a route that followed the Atchison, Topeka & Santa Fe Railroad westward, through La Junta, Colorado; Raton, New Mexico; Albuquerque, New Mexico; Flagstaff, Arizona; Needles, California; and on to my final destination, Los Angeles.

CHAPTER TWO

After their return from Marceline, Walt and Roy dedicated themselves once more to the condition of the slowly advancing construction work in the heart of the state of Florida. In the course of the last three years, thousands of acres of land had been bought up in and around the small town of Orlando. At first, no one knew who the new landowner was. It was only near the end of the acquisitions that a chain of indiscretions revealed the identity of the company that had been amassing territory piece by piece, swamp ground after swamp ground, since the summer of 1963. At that point, the owners of the last outstanding pieces of real estate charged fantastic sums, more or less a hundred times the going rate before.

Walt and Roy had conducted themselves like generals in enemy terrain. Huge maps hung on their office walls, and every new acquisition was marked by a little yellow flag; missing plots had red lines drawn around them. Between Orlando and Kissimmee the largest pleasure park in the world was coming into being, where the brothers were determined not to repeat any of the mistakes they had made because of the lack of space in Los Angeles. Since the opening of the park in Anaheim, eleven years before, the area around Disneyland, outside the gates, had been turned into a kind of second Las Vegas. Spreading like cancer were the chains of hotels, motels, restaurants, and cafes; more and more photo shops; souvenir, toy, and clothes shops; snack bars; beauty salons; and gas stations and car rental agencies. "We should have bought much more land!" Walt was enraged that his kingdom was held in an ever-tighter grip. "We should have bought up all the orange groves of Anaheim, and grown and grown, and then this would never have happened to us." The site of Disney World would occupy twice the area of Manhattan—in the fall of 1966, a jungle-like piece of land was churned over by hundreds of bulldozers, and turned into thousands of holes in the ground. Completion, according to internal memos, could not be expected before the summer of 1969.

At the same time, in mid-September 1966, Walt viewed the earliest rough sketches for the *Jungle Book* on a Moviola. Rudyard Kipling's Shere Khan, the tiger, and Bagheera, the panther, were taking shape, and Frank Thomas had just begun to provide Baloo, the bear, with his warm-hearted, comical, good nature. Ollie Johnston and Ken Andersen were the other members of Thomas's team. Walt left the little projection room with the words: "Thank you all. You've done fantastic work." News of Disney's praise spread rapidly; it hardly ever happened that the boss praised his men unambiguously. There was astonishment on all the floors of the Burbank studio—wasn't it one of Walt's best-known traits to give everyone who worked for him the feeling that he hadn't quite given his all, suggesting to each animator that he was capable of working harder, better, more precisely, more originally? And if he did happen to show his appreciation, then it was only ever obliquely—telling someone of someone else's surprisingly good work. Implying thereby that he should look to his laurels. This time, though, it was all different. Walt had given the team working on the *Jungle Book* direct and heartfelt praise.

*

After eating an early supper, as usual in front of the TV—it was Sunday, September 18—Walt told his wife he would have to go to an unforeseen meeting. The poached salmon, the deep-frozen vegetables, the potato croquettes, he barely touched. He seemed to have no appetite whatsoever.

Lillian reacted unexpectedly. "You want to go out now, at eight o'clock?"

Complications, he claimed, had come up in connection with the last of the land deals in Florida.

"Sunday was always, always a day for *us*, Walt. You promised you would at least take Sundays off. Take care of yourself, it's what I've been begging you to do for years. On Sunday evenings at least?"

"I'd much rather stay home, believe me, sit in my armchair, read one or two scripts, go to bed early . . ."

"If your meeting really is as important as all that, why don't you ask the others to come here?"

He seemed insecure, and reacted with irritation. No, he couldn't do that. There were too many others involved.

"Well, then, take me with you," Lillian insisted. "I want to be with you, you've been so . . . frail for these past weeks."

"Frail? I'm in perfect health."

"I think you shouldn't go without me."

It took some time before he succeeded in dispelling his wife's worries, giving her recurring reproaches the slip.

He steered his midnight-blue Mercedes Coupe 230 SL north up the San Diego Freeway, then turned east on Ventura, until he got to the Golden State Freeway, which he stayed on, north again, to his destination. I love my wife as much as ever, even after forty years of marriage, he thought as he drove. And I hate her just as much, too.

A half an hour's drive from his home in Holmby Hills, a sector of Beverly Hills, to Burbank, in the north of unending Los Angeles. He reached the studio after closing time, at a little before nine. The two guards stood to attention like soldiers when they saw him, opened the large electric gate of the main entrance, and saluted as they would an army general.

The moon shone very bright that night. Out of the studio windows there was a view of the jagged range of the nearby San Gabriel Mountains. Walt's shadow skipped from wall to wall as he marched down the long corridors of the oceanliner-sized building. The walls and clean floors had a pale gleam in the shimmer of the night sky. From the beginning, Walt had been in the habit of going through his draftsmen's drawings after they'd gone home. Knowing this, they were very careful what sketches they left out on their desks. But on that night, he walked past all the dark, deserted offices, without looking into a single one of them.

Hazel George was waiting for him in the laughing room. Took him in her arms, without a word. Held him tight, very tight. Ten candles flickered gently, there was no other light.

"Why ten candles?" he asked.

"We haven't seen each other in ten days . . ."

"I'm sorry . . . I didn't have a moment . . ."

"Your favorite dish is waiting for you," Hazel told him. "It'll only take a couple of minutes to heat up."

"Chili con carne?"

"Combine one Heinz can: not much meat, lots of beans, with one Dennison can: lots of meat, not many beans." She stroked Walt's cheek, kissed him on the forehead. He would take his favorite food with him on trips, fill half a suitcase with cans, and then, in London's Dorchester Hotel, for instance, ask the liveried waiter to heat up the food he'd brought. Though by no means a vegetarian, he couldn't stand to see red meat, much less eat it. Beef and lamb and pork had to be prepared in such a way that there wasn't the least trace of blood. Poultry could not be served whole, but only jointed and boned, so that such things as legs and wings couldn't be identified. Fish he would only tolerate without the head, and carefully filleted.

He sat down on the black leather couch. Fished a plastic comb from his trouser pocket, combed his iron gray hair straight back. Poured himself a large tumbler of whiskey, and drank it greedily. "Hazel?"

"Yes, my angel?"

"I . . . I'm in a lot of pain . . ."

"We'll get started on that right away. We haven't seen each other for a long while, don't you forget that."

"I don't like it when you watch me, when I feel so much pain . . ."

"If you like, we can play Hangman after supper? Or Battleship?"

"I like Scrabble better."

"Because you always win!"

A gigantic color TV, a Zenith, especially made that size for Walt, stood in a corner of the room. Plugged into an internal studio transmitter, it put out nothing but film of U.S. space missions. Rockets taking off, earth orbits, space walks, docking maneuvers, the rendezvous of two manned Gemini capsules. Pictures, flickering across the screen, all of them silent. He stared at the TV, both tired and fascinated. In Washington, a few weeks ago, he had attended a banquet to celebrate the successful conclusion of the Gemini project. John Glenn and Edwin Aldrin, Neil Armstrong and James Lovell, Michael Collins and Charles Conrad, and many of their space colleagues had come on President Johnson's invitation. All those present had clustered around Walt. It was to him that the assembled guests gave the most attention. Far more than to Johnson. More than to any of the astronauts. The journalists present and the space pilots and their wives and their children, their siblings, and uncles and aunts all had begged Walt for autographs.

"Armstrong," he said to Hazel, stretching out his tormenting right leg, "one of the best NASA pilots, Neil Armstrong, I recently called Wernher von Braun to request that Armstrong be the first man on the moon."

"Why Armstrong, Walt?" asked Hazel, even though space travel didn't especially interest her.

"Because he gave me his word, but you're to keep this to yourself, Hazel, he said that on the first moon landing he would leave a Mickey doll and a copy of the very first Mickey film, *Plane Crazy*, in the Sea of Silence. With my signature on Mickey's back. Nobody is supposed to know. He swore on the life of his parents. I like Neil. An Ohio country boy. And I'm impressed by the way he can look into the future and describe the mission: 'Walt,' he said to me, 'I can see the whole thing very clearly: the earth will look like a marble, a tiny, beautiful blue marble. I'll close one eye, and hold my thumb up in front of the other one and block out the whole planet. But it won't make me feel godlike or anything like that, Walt. At that moment, I know I'll feel very very small.'"

Hazel was convinced it would be another fifty years at least before man landed on the moon.

"Long before that, my dear, in two or three years," insisted Walt. "I want to be alive to see it."

"Why in God's name shouldn't you be alive to see it?"

"I'm scared . . ."

"Name one dream of yours that hasn't been fulfilled . . ."

"Having you as my wife."

"Oh, I can hear the violins, you schmaltzy man."

"I mean it."

"You will live to see the moon landing, my friend. Here, shake hands— I give you my word."

Walt had hired the rocket engineer Wernher von Braun as a consultant in 1951, and asked him, together with one of his best studio artists, Ward Kimball, and another German physicist, Heinz Haber, to make a semidocumentary for TV. The program would demonstrate that traveling to the moon was becoming a real possibilty. So, in the mid-fifties, about the time Walt took me on, "Man and the Moon" was broadcast and provoked great interest. How proud I was to be able to say, "The people who made that show are friends of mine. The dream factory I belong to puts out the most beautiful, happiest, most entertaining, most informative films and books and comics in the world. We produce mass culture— but with style and power and originality."

"Eisenhower called Walt the morning after the program aired," recalled Heinz Haber almost thirty years later, when I went to visit him at his summer chalet in Seefeld in the Tirol. "The president asked us to loan him a copy of 'Man and the Moon' to show to his generals, those stuffed shirts in the Pentagon, who seemed obsessed with conducting war in the most old-fashioned manner; so they spent weeks studying our film about going to the moon, which we had basically put together for children. Only three months later the White House announced the surprising plan to send satellites into orbit in the near future. I wrote to von Braun to say that our film had been crucial in influencing the president. This worried Wernher: he was deeply concerned about his reputation as a scientist. For God's sake, he asked Ward Kimball and me, please don't make it appear as though our cartoon show had spurred the president's announcement!"

"Why shouldn't you live to see a man land on the moon?" Hazel repeated her question.

"I'm so proud, Hazel, so endlessly proud of everything I've achieved. And at the same time, I feel a kind of fear that I haven't felt for years. As though something were lurking, lying in wait for me ..."

"I don't know what you're talking about."

"I can feel something ... gnawing at me and tiring me out."

"Lie down, come on, I'll give you a massage."

"I'd rather you gave me a foot rub, darling."

"I've got a better idea. First we'll eat something, and then I'll massage your feet."

She went into the tiny kitchen, where the chili con carne was simmering on the wood stove. She brought in the large copper saucepan, and they both ate from it with tin soupspoons. That was the way Walt liked it—the same as in Marceline, when he and his siblings ate their meals, all from the same pot. He told Hazel about his visit to his former home, of the crowd that had gathered around him wherever he showed up. He spoke fondly of his return to the sources of his childhood.

"You should visit Marceline more often—not just once every ten years!"

"From now on I'm going to go every year. That's a decision I've made."

"Go in spring, when the trees are in bloom."

"I've got some big plans."

"You get a lot of snow in Missouri!" Hazel came from Montana. Like Walt she had grown up on a farm. She had missed the seasons ever since she'd moved to California over a quarter of a century ago. He urged her to visit her home more often. Since her mother's death (her father had died when she was only a girl), she had seen no reason ever to go back to the village of New Florence. Only her desire to see, to sniff, snow-covered mountains, meadows, and woods, to feel snow on her hands, sometimes made her feel sad.

I got to know Hazel George in early 1967, at the house of Aron Silverstein, a doctor who had treated Disney the previous fall. She wore a stark white uniform, with a red and blue Mickey Mouse pin where nurses usually wear a red cross. For twenty-five years, Walt Disney had regarded her as his only confidante. He believed his confessions would remain safe with her, that she would take them with her to the grave. As soon as I sensed this, I did everything I could to get close to her. Without ever being aware of it, she ended up betraying her patient and friend more profoundly than anyone else he knew. I made her repeat several times every seemingly insignificant detail; there were certain scenes and conversations and instants I kept going back to over and over again. I often drove her mad with my interrogations, and frequently she would order me to leave her house and never come back again. Then I would give her one of her favorite things, a bar of Swiss chocolate from the firm of Frigor, or a bottle of the sweet liqueur Benedictine, and I'd be restored to her good graces. And started tormenting her again, spreading out her experiences with Walt on the dissecting table. I often wonder why Hazel ever allowed me to do that.

That night, Walt ate his chili con carne with appetite. "I'm dreading the garden party that Lillian's planning," he observed, sticking his spoon to the bottom of the pot. "It's supposed to be a birthday surprise. Of course, I am aware of the preparations. It's unavoidable. Yesterday, the president sent word he's coming. It's because of him she started sending out the invitations, almost a year ago. This is so embarrassing to me."

"I can't wait to meet Johnson in the flesh."

"A coward!" scolded Walt. "Bombing the Vietcong back into the Middle Ages, *that* would be a nice present for my sixty-fifth birthday. But instead L.B.J.'s a slave to the liberal establishment in this country. He should have mined the North Vietnamese ports, marched into Cambodia and Thailand, whipped the whole damned region into shape. We've got hundreds of thousands of men fighting there—I don't get it, we should have beat them years ago. But with marijuana and whores and the *New York Times* undermining you every day, how can you do a good job? Why do you think I supported Goldwater? So he'd finish off the Communists!"

"That clown must have taken you to the cleaners."

"I can't believe my Hazel's a Democrat! Now there's proof of my affection, letting a damned traitor like you anywhere near me. Well, he did suffer the worst electoral defeat in the history of the U.S.A., my friend Barry, didn't he? But Ronald Reagan's another story—I'm sure he's going to be elected governor two months from now. I'm not going to take my eyes off Reagan, he could even be president one day. And he's putty in my hands. For years he's been taking my advice, how to present himself, how to speak, how to move. I was the one who talked him out of his left-wing beliefs, you know Ron used to be a Democrat, like you, and on the very left of the party at that! Today we're thick as thieves. I've contributed as much money to his campaign as I did to Goldwater's back in '64. I'm going to see that Reagan goes all the way. I'm going to look after him, Hazel, like a mother looks after her child."

"How do you like your chili today?"

"It's incredibly good. I like it so much better, Hazel bunny, than all those fancy dishes they serve me at home. Before, I used to be able to go down to Musso & Frank's, and order my favorite dishes. But today? No thanks. It's gotten really bad since my TV show, since the Mickey Mouse

Club, since they've started beaming me into every household in the country. I can't imagine going into a restaurant now! How I long to be able to lead a normal life again, at least once in a while. How dreadful to go out in public and have everyone stare at me as if I'd just climbed out of a flying saucer. And they always ask the same stupid questions, too. I can't do anything I really want to do. Can't smoke in public. Can't go in a bar and drink a whiskey. I'd love to produce a film like *To Kill a Mockingbird* ... but it's all impossible. The one time I tried to put a vaguely erotic scene in a movie ...."

"*Bon Voyage* ... ?"

"*Bon Voyage*, exactly ... all because Fred MacMurray got wrapped up in a goddamned conversation with a goddamned whore. I got bags and bags of letters from angry parents. How could I be so immoral. Disney stood for clean fun, kids, no hidden meanings. I can't ever do the things I really want to do."

"My poor, poor darling!"

"You're making fun of me. I'm warning you: my technicians will soon be able to build a robot that can massage me."

"And will it cook? And love you? Will it be able to do those things as well?"

"Sure. Just give them one or two more years."

"I wasn't making fun of you."

"Just lately, I haven't been able to shake off the feeling that my name isn't my own any longer. It's still my name of course, but really it belongs to the company. To a company that goes everywhere using my name. Am I me, or am I a company? In fifty years, if the studio still exists, no one will know there was a living human being behind it, one Walter Elias Disney. They'll think that Walt Disney, those three magic syllables, are a brand, no different from Campbell's, or Westinghouse Electric, or Ford Motors, or Howard Johnson's ...."

He closed his eyes. Leaned back. Lit a cigarette, the next to last in the day's third pack of Luckies. "Ah, that tasted so good! Thank you!"

Hazel knelt down at Walt's feet that were resting on a footstool. She began rubbing his soles.

"Oh God, that's so painful, Hazel, that spot there ... ooh ..."

"You're healthy, completely healthy, I know that for a fact," she murmured, "but I want you to promise me you'll stop smoking. That'll cure your cough at long last. And you mustn't drink so much!"

"That's two strikes—I'm waiting for the third."

"I want you to get yourself examined by a good doctor I know."

"Never."

Hazel could be very strict. Later on, I was to discover that for myself. She let go of his feet, stood up, ready to walk out on him.

He gave in immediately. "All right, arrange a time, I'll go. Goddamned doctors—quacks, charlatans, every last one of them!"

"Tomorrow?"

"Tomorrow."

"Done. Four o'clock tomorrow afternoon, you report to Dr. Silverstein. It couldn't be more convenient, he works at St. Joseph's Hospital, just across the street from the studio."

"You're just like my mother."

"Nonsense."

"How would you know? You never met her."

"I'm nothing like your mother."

"You smell like her. Talk like her. Think like her ..."

"Come on now, that's enough."

"My poor, dear mother ..." And he sank into the story of his parents' move to Los Angeles in 1939, which Hazel was subjected to repeatedly, at intervals of a few months. They left their home in Portland, Oregon, Flora and Elias, and occupied the comfortable bungalow in North Hollywood bought for them by Walt and Roy for eight thousand three hundred dollars in cash. "My parents never wanted to leave Portland. They were happy where they were. They had Ruth, my little sister, living next door. It was just us, Roy and me, insisting on having them nearer. Finally, they gave in, and moved down with all their belongings. And then just two weeks later ... Flora ...”

“Don’t think about it, Walt. Please, for my sake, stop.”

“The gas furnace, which gave us hot water as well, brand new, something was wrong with it ... And it was *me* who had chosen the damned thing. I argued for having that gas boiler, instead of another one that cost twice as much. Mama choked from poisonous gases, as the coroner told us. And I’m to blame.”

“You’re not to blame, Walt.”

“Well, who else?”

“It all happened such a long time ago, twenty-seven years ...”

“... And still I feel as though it had all happened only yesterday. Do you think Flora might have turned it up deliberately, so that all that poison leaked out? Do you think that’s possible? But why would she have done a thing like that?”

Hazel took his hands in hers. She kissed his palms.

“I ... I’m afraid, my angel,” he whispered.

“What are you afraid of?”

“... Of the other side. And of everything going on without me. My whole empire will collapse ... Without me ...”

“It’s not that you’re sick, Walt. I was just saying you should see a doctor, for a normal checkup, that’s all.”

“Mickey and Donald will live forever, Hazel, they’re immortal, just like the gods in Greek legends. Like Moses or Zeus or Jesus, like Mohammed and Buddha. More children know Mickey than Christ, who would ever have thought that? Mickey ... and Donald! But what about my parents? And Lillian? And my children and grandchildren? And you, Hazel? You, all of you must ... die! We all must. Die. *I* will have to die ... I can’t believe it. Ever since I’ve been able to think for myself, I haven’t been able to grasp that people really, really ... die ...”

“Stretch out, we’ll play the body game,” she commanded.

"Not today, love, not today, I can't."

"Shut your eyes. Name the first animal you see."

He was still protesting, even as he slowly stretched out on the chaise longue.

"Then I won't play Scrabble with you."

Reluctantly, he gave in.

"Name the first animal," she insisted, "you see."

"A squirrel . . . But with *white* fur, which is strange."

"Put it in your head, your squirrel with white fur," demanded Hazel, "and look at your brain, the back of your eyes, the inside of your ears . . . Check if everything's all right."

"I'm cold, Hazel, I'm awfully cold."

She covered him with a soft angora wool blanket, a large motif of an Indian chief in a splendid feather headdress woven into it. That blanket has belonged to me since my thirty-first birthday. Hazel gave it to me. I'm looking at it now behind me on the couch, as I read the proofs of the present book, in my small house in the Hollywood Hills. I see it lying there, half in sunlight, the same blanket, the same soft warm blanket. It's red, green, yellow, white, and blue. It's still very beautiful.

"And now take your squirrel down, go down your throat into your chest with it, tell me what you see there . . ."

He didn't want to go on with the game. "The heart's all right," he said anyway, "it's beating regularly. The veins and capillaries look healthy to me, I can't see anything wrong there . . . The lungs, though . . . They certainly don't look good, the right lung-tip, no, the left . . . Doesn't look good, Hazel, it doesn't look good at all, now please let's stop, I hate this damn game."

"Go on, Walt, what else does your squirrel see?"

He was bitterly cold, even with the blanket over him. "My jugular feels like an icicle, that's how cold I am, Hazel. I'm shivering. Please help me, help me, can't you see I . . . I'm *freezing to death?*" He jumped up. Ran next door, to the oven. He pressed himself against the stove, as once in the kitchen in Marceline, in midwinter, let the warmth flow through his belly and hips.

"I've rarely felt as terrifically cold in my entire life, Hazel, but it's given me an amazing idea. Come here, my little dove." How he could call her a little dove, I am still wondering, years later, she was the least dove-like creature imaginable. "I've found the answer," he was squeezing her to him in the kitchenette. "If I should have to die, then I won't be buried in an ordinary graveyard. Instead I'll have myself put on ice. Until the day people can cure diseases that to us are still incurable. Or death has been abolished altogether. Then they can thaw me out, whether it's in fifty or hundred or five hundred years. I can wait . . . Then again, there are so many things that need to be done now. That's what scares me the most, having to leave before finishing everything I've set myself to do. Maybe they can manage resurrection before the century's out? Science is advancing with leaps and bounds, perhaps they'll be able to cure every disease before the millennium. Then I might be back in your lifetime!"

"You really are a child," she replied.

"I don't think you quite understand, Hazel. I'm going to have myself deep-frozen, damn it. For some years, they've been able to perform the most incredible experiments, I just never thought of having this technology, cryonics, applied to myself. Curious isn't it. Until today. Until now." While working on the futuristic city he was planning for Disney World in Florida, with the working title of EPCOT, an acronym for Experimental Prototype Community of Tomorrow, he came across a great number of writings that dealt with the future possibilities of prolonging life. He had been particularly struck by one book that his friend, the science-fiction author Ray Bradbury had recommended, *The Prospect of Immortality* by Robert Ettinger. "Even today," he read, "it is theoretically possible to preserve a corpse in liquid nitrogen for an indefinite period—without doing it any harm. If civilization endures, medical science should eventually be able to repair almost any damage to the human body, including freezing damage and senile debility or any other cause of death. Hence we need only arrange to have our bodies, after we die, stored in suitable freezers against the time when science may be able to help us. No matter what kills us, whether old age or disease, and even if freezing techniques are still crude when we die, sooner or later our friends of the future should be equal to the task of reviving and curing us. The arrangements will no doubt be handled at first by individuals, then by private companies, and perhaps later by the Social Security system."

Rats and mice, dogs and cats had been successfully frozen and thawed out in the mid-sixties, always in a matter of hours after being clinically dead. The bigger the community of scientists who undertook serious research in the possibilities of cryobiology, such was Walt's conviction, the sooner the possibility of a rebirth after years or decades in ice, at temperatures of minus one hundred and fifty Farenheit, would become a reality.

He had never been willing to think about his mortality, but now, animated by the conviction that he had made one of the most important decisions of his life, he sailed in the opposite direction: "My so-called coffin, a smooth metal container, will be kept deep underground, Hazel, either in Orlando or else here, under the studio, or in Anaheim, under the Pirates of the Caribbean, as in a deep glacial crevasse, and there I'll wait until I'm thawed out . . . And healed." It was this moment that I kept returning to with Hazel in later years, the instant in which he gave his closest confidante the awkward assignment of one day having to work to turn his desire into fact: "You're my great hope. You will be responsible for making sure everything goes the way I want it to!"

"But I *can't* do that! They'll want to bury you . . . I'm sorry, but your family's bound to do whatever they want, and not what I ask them to do."

"I'm making you and Roy responsible for carrying out my last wish. You two and my best technician, Phil Bowman, whom I'm going to confide in tomorrow, you three will be the only ones informed. I truly see myself as the founder of a new type of burial, and when I have myself frozen, this form of farewell will become fashionable all over the world. I'll become a kind of Messiah for everyone who is afraid of death, just you wait, you'll live to see it happening. Your friend Walt will have started a new religion. . . . I still need to talk Roy into it, my project would have no chance of success without him, I think you're right about that. Roy and I, we're as close as a pair of goddamned testicles. My big brother, who always did the right and sensible thing. Then again, how many times he used to tell me my ideas were stupid, and even tried to shoot some of them down. How often he refused to raise money for my very best projects. Everyone sees him as the brilliant financier of our company. And yet his first objective was always saving money. And paying back our debts. His lack of courage was limitless at times. But then again: without him, we wouldn't have amounted to anything. Without him I would have been lost."

"I know, Walt."

"Listen to me. Listen very carefully. Don't change the subject. Look me in the eye when I'm talking. I can't stand people who look away when I'm speaking to them."

"I'm sorry . . ."

"Roy's my big brother, I've always wanted to impress him. He ran away from home, from Kansas City, when I was ten and he was seventeen. Like Herbert, he had had enough of being beaten by our dad. And apart from him, who have I got? Only you. I've got Roy and I've got you."

"And Lillian and Diane and Sharon."

"Compared to you two, complete strangers."

"You have your friends . . ."

"They're not worth mentioning."

"I'm afraid . . . I won't be able to do anything for you . . ."

"Hazel, once more. You and Roy—Roy if he's still alive then—are responsible for my last wish, which is the deepest wish I've ever had."

Hazel had to promise that she would do everything in her power to see to it that Walt Disney's body would one day be deep frozen in liquid nitrogen. But she added in a firm voice: "You're going to live for many more years, Walt, believe me. You'll outlive your brother. He's seventy-two, and you're turning sixty-five in three months. So there. Stop thinking about all that stuff."

"You've got to swear that you're going to help me. I know you can't do it by yourself. So, I'll have to talk to doctors, involve some technicians. There'll be a lot of paperwork to take care of. But I want to be able to depend on you. Will you swear that you will make absolutely sure that my wishes are respected?

She swore she would. "Now that's enough of that . . ."

"Swear it to me by the flag of the United States of America."

"I swear by the flag of the United States of America."

On the television monitor, a gigantic rocket was waiting for liftoff. The engines lit, spewed clouds of snow-white gases into the air. He pointed to an image of the flag on the body of the Saturn booster, demanded that Hazel set her hand on the flag to make her vow.

Hazel knelt down, pressed her palm against the lower left portion of the television screen which crackled with static. And once more she repeated the words: "I swear by the flag of the United States of America."

CHAPTER THREE

"Lincoln's giving us all kinds of problems, Walt, sir. Today's Saturday, tomorrow's our busiest day in the week. I'm very worried. You're the only one who can deal with the president. This afternoon, he wrecked two of his official chairs, sir, Walt." Chuck Amen, the chief technician at Disneyland, got his boss on the telephone, asked if he might pick him up at his house and drive him to Anaheim.

Six days had passed since the night that Walt had promised Hazel he would go to St. Joseph's Hospital to have himself examined by Dr. Silverstein. He did not keep his word. Occupied himself instead, almost entirely, with questions of cryobiology—much to the frustration of several of his key men, who needed to consult him on a whole range of matters on a daily basis, having to do with the great building site in Orlando. Walt, meanwhile, kept requesting more and more publications, scientific periodicals, and works of imagination from all over the country and abroad, all on the theme of cryotechnology, insisting that this branch of research would turn out to be critical to the planned EPCOT undertaking. He informed Roy the following day on his newest inspiration. Tried to make an ally of him—urged his brother to take steps on his own behalf, to make early preparations to have himself deep frozen when the time came. His elder brother reacted with a furious shake of the head. But Walt wasn't to be deterred; after all, when had it been any other way. First the rejection, even the condemnation of new suggestions, proposals, and ideas, followed by the gradual understanding that Walt was right after all, and he, Roy, had been wrong.

He all but neglected the *Jungle Book*, except for the little hilarious dance he did in the corridor for Ollie Johnston, the film's chief animator, who immediately committed to paper Walt's wobble, his hands waving like a penguin's wings at chest height, and so immortalized it in the cheery strides of the good-humored bear Baloo. With that one exception, the great inspirer, as his admirers called him, left all artistic, dramaturgical, and organizational decisions to the team of Johnston, Andersen, and Thomas: "Oh, I don't know, fellas, you guys carry on. At the moment, I'm bored with cartoons. Please spare me the details. I liked what you showed me ten days ago. I've got other things on my mind. Do your business to your usual standards, and I'll be satisfied."

The nine old men, as Walt liked to refer to Les Clark, Marc Davis, Oliver Johnston, Milt Kahl, Ward Kimball, Eric Larson, John Lounsbery, Wolfgang Reitherman, and Frank Thomas, in an allusion to the nine judges on the United States Supreme Court, in other words, his most trusted, longest-serving cartoon animators, who had been with him since the days of *Snow White*, held an urgent meeting. They concluded that Walt was going through a serious crisis, not unlike the nervous breakdown, caused by acute overwork, that had taken him to the brink of suicide in 1931. Johnston, their leader, tried to talk to Lillian, to persuade her that her husband was not quite himself at the moment and needed to take a break, or go away somewhere.

Lillian didn't listen to the old men's counsel.

In those days, Walt and his wife were deeply at odds. Often, when he got home, she would be asleep, or out with one of their daughters, occasionally spending the night at Diane's house. The weekend that Chuck Amen called, Lillian had gone off to the ranch in Palm Springs, with two of Diane's six children, Tamara and Walter.

Nor did Hazel know anything about the nocturnal mission to rescue Abraham Lincoln. It wasn't until the next day that she found out what had happened.

Walt heard the crunch of wheels on the gravel drive. From a pine chest that had been in his wife's family for generations, he got a pair of blue jeans, some cowboy boots, and a checkered flannel shirt that he normally wore for gardening. He put on his broadest-brimmed hat, and walked out to meet Chuck Amen, moving easily and lightly. As he climbed into the Cadillac limousine late on the evening of September 24, 1966, he felt stronger and fitter than he had in a long time.

Driving down to Anaheim (forty miles south on the San Diego Freeway, as far as Rossmoor, and then following the Garden Grove Freeway for some fifteen miles east), the obese and very shy engineer told him about the difficulties that had arisen in the course of the afternoon with the Abraham Lincoln doll. It had become as uncontrollable as two years before, when the studio had first built the audio-animatronics machine for the Illinois pavillion of the New York World's Fair. The idea of building a simulacrum of the most popular of all American presidents, the savior of the Union, had been Walt's. The task of bringing the electric scarecrow to life, he left to Steve Berthold and Wathel Rogers, the pair of technical geniuses who had been responsible for a great number of Disneyland's attractions. From the start, the newly built automaton was much more lifelike than, say, the wax dolls at Madame Tussaud's. The surface of its rubber cheeks began to sweat and glisten under the heat of the spotlights. All its limbs were movable, the head alone was able to perform eighteen separate movements, the body forty-nine. It shifted its mechanical weight in such a realistic way from one leg to another that, when I visited the New York World's Fair with my wife and my two then infant sons, I couldn't suppress the feeling that I was really seeing a dead man brought back to life. The automaton broke down fairly frequently in the first weeks of testing; on three occasions, members of the technical staff were injured when the machine went haywire and failed to respond to any of the remote controls. A Belgian stagehand was wounded on the chin, and fled America the moment he was released from the hospital's emergency room. These incidents were all hushed up, such was the pressure that this General Electric–funded sensation appear as an unqualified success.

Walt was the only one who could control the figure, at a time when even its constructors were ready to throw in the towel. Something approaching hero-worship began to spread among the workers and technicians. Because each time Walt spoke to the deranged Lincoln doll on the stage of the General Electric Pavillion of the New York World's Fair, spent a few minutes alone with it, the automaton gradually calmed down and reverted to its normal behavior—said its stored sentences in the correct, preprogrammed sequence, behaved, in short, as though there had never been any unfortunate complications.

*

It was half past ten by the time Walt and Chuck reached the town of Anaheim in Orange County, over fifty miles southeast of Holmby Hills, twice as far as the studios in Burbank to the north, and yet still part of greater metropolitan Los Angeles. Amen had a special permit to take the limousine into the Magic Kingdom, where automobiles were generally not allowed. They stopped and got out on the dimly lit Main Street. The street sweepers had done their work. A strange scene, the cobbled street without the throng and din of mothers, fathers, children, grandparents, uncles, aunts, and godparents. Without the balloon sellers and popcorn stands, without the piping of the carousel organs. More than fifty million people had visited Walt's kingdom in the eleven years since its opening in mid-July 1955. What a dreamlike scene, this depopulated Main Street! He often treated himself to the secret pleasure of seeing it like this; there were reports of him creeping through the streets of his empire at three or four a.m.

Above the fire station, roughly halfway down Main Street on the left-hand side, he had had a little furnished apartment made for himself, a red plush saloon whose fittings consisted of antique pieces from the early 1880s: a chaise longue and a couple of armchairs, also in red plush, a commode, a little table, a lofty mirror, an enamel basin. He used to stay over in this little hideaway sometimes, on evenings when he felt out of sorts and preferred to be on his own.

He asked Chuck in to have a drink with him in his little apartment. Amen was a Mormon, and refused the invitation with firmness, almost rudeness. Disappointed, Walt got out the silver flask he kept upstairs in a drawer, filled it with whiskey, and went back down to the silent street.

They walked the few steps to the entrance of the attraction, "Great Moments with Mister Lincoln," next to the barber's shop. Chuck pulled a heavy bunch of keys from his briefcase, opened the door's four locks, before they stepped into the pitch dark. There was a smell of sweat, dust, and bleach.

"Amen, I want you to get rid of this awful smell by tomorrow."

The employee turned on the main switch. All the lights came on simultaneously over the stage and in the large auditorium, dazzling the two men.

"We've tried everything, sir, to get rid of . . ."

"I'm certain you haven't tried *everything*."

"It's also a question of money . . ."

"I don't want any false economies."

"I'll see what I can do."

"That's not good enough, Chuck. You'll have to do more than that. A lot more. And that goes for everything you want to achieve in life."

"I understand, Walt, sir."

"I don't need all this light, Amen."

"Shall I just keep the little one on overhead?"

"That'll be fine . . ."

One light remained on, high above the stage, not more than forty watts.

On a lofty chair of state sat the life-sized doll, made of rubber, metal, cloth and hair, glass, and wood. Upright, proud, and silent. Its suit was woven from the finest fabrics, the black tailcoat of a mixture of silk and cotton, the dazzling white dress shirt freshly pressed, every three or four days the clothes washed, the shoes polished, the cuff-links burnished, the socks and tie replaced.

On the left was a round table with quill pen, paper and blotter, and next to it, very noticeable, a Stars and Stripes. On the right an old-fashioned globe held in a wooden frame.

Walt took off his cowboy hat, and slowly, carefully approached Abraham Lincoln, bowing low to him as to an idol.

Amen turned on a small tape recorder, one of the earliest portable cassette players available. He concealed it under the stage, let it run unnoticed. Chuck, with whom I was to become friendly in later years, gave me permission to use the tapes for my research. He calls me an overly enthusiastic fanatic, a man with a dependency on a drug called Walter Elias Disney. He has a point.

"Order up some new eyes, Amen," Walt is heard impatiently calling to his employee, "this present pair look used up. Hasn't anyone noticed?" In San Pablo in the vicinity of San Francisco there was an enterprise that went by the name of Eye-and-You that specialized in the making of glass eyes. Owned by Lillian's first cousin, Robert Bounds, and supplying principally Californian eye clinics, the company had been dangerously close to bankruptcy since the mid-50s, due to Asian competition. A few months before the opening of Disneyland, the little factory had the greatest boom in its history: for the Caribbean Pirates display alone, two hundred and fifty pairs of eyes were required immediately, and they would need to be replaced on an annual basis. The advance orders for the numerous audio-animatronic installations in the rest of the park, also requiring annual replacement, made Eye-and-You one of the most profitable companies of its kind.

For some minutes all that can be heard on the tape is the creaking of the wooden boards, until a young man's voice says over the public address system: "To respect the dignity of the moment, we request you to refrain from taking pictures. Thank you."

Abraham Lincoln rose from his chair of state, took three or four steps, put his right hand to his temple, and let it fall again. And spoke the first of the sentences stored in a maze of cables and little transistors: "My countrymen, if you have been taught doctrines conflicting with those great landmarks of the Declaration of Independence, if you have listened to suggestions that would take away its grandeur, if you are inclined to believe that all men are not created equal, let me entreat you to come back. Come back to the truths that are in the Declaration of Independence. Do not destroy that immortal emblem of humanity."

The voice was Kirk Douglas's. It was only after long hesitation that the actor had agreed to speak the text of the Lincoln machine; to Douglas, the making of this legendary figure was practically blasphemous. Walt invited him and his sons, Michael and Eric, to his house, and let them take rides for over an hour on the model train set up in the garden of the villa in Holmby Hills. The locomotive and cars, scaled down to 1:8, circled round and round the property. The engine was powerful, the roofs of the toy cars strong enough to be sat on with knees drawn up. The visitors enjoyed their tour of the garden very much indeed. And a few days later, Walt sent Kirk one of the most expensive watches from the Swiss manufacturer Patek Philippe, an automatic, golden Calatrava. Finally, he achieved his objective: a few weeks after visiting Disney in Holmby Hills, Douglas gave the Lincoln doll his own unmistakable voice.

"Come back," Walt declaimed in unison with the doll, "to the truths that are in the Declaration of Independence. Do not destroy that immortal emblem of humanity." Then Walt: "That's right. Faultless. Word perfect. Then how does it go? Mr. President? Please . . . Would you carry on?"

Over the stage in large red letters was the sign: NO SMOKING! Walt lit himself a cigarette. Drew the smoke deep into himself. Reached for the silver flask, and took a swig.

"This afternoon, he got stuck in exactly the same place," Amen can be heard saying. "He seems to manage the opening sentence without any trouble, sir, but then . . ."

"You know, Chuck, I have sometimes had to fire people for continuing to call me sir, instead of Walt, so I would watch out if I were you."

"It won't happen again."

"Come over here. Come on, I want to tell you something. You know, the photographs we have of Lincoln? They're all misleading. There he was sitting in the photographer's studio, not allowed to move a single muscle for minutes on end, it wasn't possible to take pictures any other way in those days, the subject had to stay absolutely still. So we don't have a single picture that shows us anything of Lincoln's wonderful vivacity."

"That's a terrific description, sir, Walt . . ."

"Then again, some contemporaries describe his body language as cumbersome, and his movements as slow and lethargic. Like a machine that needs oil. A lot of his contemporaries thought of him as gangling, and his long arms and legs continually seemed to get in his way."

"Just like his model, sir, Walt . . ."

"Will you leave me alone with him for a while."

"All . . . alone?"

"Yeah. All alone."

"You want to be careful, sir, please!"

"I'll give a sign, Chuck, if I need help."

"I really don't want to leave you on your own . . ."

He retreated into a little room behind the stage. He looked down through an airshaft, observed every movement of his boss's dealings with the robot.

"Mr. President," whispered Walt, "please will you carry on."

Lincoln did as he was asked: "The world has never had a good definition of the word *liberty*, and the American people, just now, are much in want of one. We all declare for liberty; but in using the same word we do not all mean the same thing. Thing. Thing. Thing . . ."

With the plastic comb that he always carried, like a trucker or fairground barker, in his back pocket, Walt combed the doll's coarse beard and bushy eyebrows, both made from genuine human hair. Then he opened a little panel in the doll's shoulder, fiddled with the dials, and tinkered with some wires.

"Not long ago, I undertook another pilgrimage to your statue in Washington, D.C.," he murmured into the large ear. "I stood before your marble effigy in Constitution Gardens. And I cried like a baby. To see you sitting there! On your throne! Your long arms, your majestic hands on the armrests of the broad stone seat—so upright and proud! What a miraculous piece of sculpture! I visited you on the same day that President Johnson gave me the Freedom Medal at the White House. When I was nine—how many times have I told you this already?—I recited your Gettysburg Address in school by heart. I had put on father's battered top hat and dusty tailcoat. To think that he let me borrow those things! It was purely because he idolized you. Daddy was only six when you died, and that gave him the feeling of having known you, if only in the most distant and indirect sort of way: you were president when he was a little boy. I was such a good Abe Lincoln that Cottingham, the principal, made me perform in front of every single class. Got me to repeat my performance dozens of times. A ritual carried on until the time I left school, at fourteen. From then on I never saw the inside of a school building again. Not until my daughter started. You know, even now I can't spell properly, that's what I have secretaries for. But anything that anyone's ever told me, or anything I've ever read, even once, stays with me all my life. I soak it all up, like a sponge."

"I am nothing. But truth is everything," Lincoln took a couple of cautious steps toward the front of the stage, his noble curved lips moving in time to his words. "And with God's help, I shall not fail—I shall not—shall not. Not. Not." And he walked stiffly backward. His features looked twisted with pain, as though he had the bullet of the assassin John Wilkes Booth still lodged in the back of his head. Gently, he sat down on his seat again.

"Chuck? Would you get me a chair please, quickly?"

Amen got one as quickly as he could, and then withdrew.

Walt ground out his cigarette butt with his heel, and sat down next to the doll. He took its finely haired rubber hand, with its dark yellow fingertips, in his own, and spoke softly, in soothing tones: "We come from the same background, you and I, Abraham; we're both sons of simple folk. Grew up on farms, in great poverty. As children, we moved several times from state to state, you really couldn't say our fathers had an easy time, did they? It was all they could do to feed their families. Your father, Thomas, and my father, Elias, seemed to be doomed to fail from the outset. When you were a boy you heard the cry of the panther in the forests of Indiana, the roar of the hunting bear, the grunting of wild boar. As a boy, like me, you caught trout in streams with your bare hands, and watched squirrels and deer, raccoons and bobcats hunting and at play, killing and being killed, and mating. We helped our anxious fathers sow and reap. As boys, we had a gift for acting, we used to mimic our teachers and our ministers. And, in spite of every obstacle, in the teeth of all opposition, both of us succeeded in making something of ourselves: more than that, we changed the world. We're folk heroes, legendary figures, you and I, Mr. President. But distinguished men like ourselves, we have enemies, that's for sure. You were in office for only four years, your second term had just begun when the assassin's bullet hit you—and in spite of that, you were the savior of the Union, the great liberator, the embodiment of the great qualities of our nation . . ."

Without getting up, Lincoln spoke quickly, far too quickly: "Slavery is a fundamental ill, or more, it's an injustice." And he said it again: "Slavery is a fundamental ill, or more, it's an injustice. Slavery is a fundamental ill, or more, it's an injustice." Froze, and fell silent.

"Mr. President, I thought we'd cut that line quite some time ago. Amen, will you come, please? Chuck?"

"Slavery," the automaton spoke up once more, "is a fundamental ill, or more, it's an injustice . . ."

"You were a notable supporter of the Negro race, that's a major difference between us. Martin Luther King? Eldridge Cleaver? Is that really what you wanted? Doesn't that go too far, even for you, what those fellows ask for?" Walt allowed the doll's hand to slip from his own, lit himself another Lucky Strike. Puffed out clouds of smoke, like steam from a locomotive. "No doubt about it, I'm always on my guard toward black people. Nor will I permit any one of them to work for me, at least I haven't yet, neither here in Anaheim nor in Burbank. I'll take one on as a gardener from time to time, and of course most of the cleaning ladies are black. But I prefer to steer clear of them. That boxer, Cassius Clay, I had to ban him from Disneyland, immediately and indefinitely. When he's among friends, he's an opponent of the Vietnam War. I heard that from reliable sources . . ."

Amen came out on stage, the boards creaked under his heavy steps. Walt didn't notice him, paid him no attention, so engrossed was he in the dialogue with his doll.

"You look like a scarecrow, Mr. President. Like a skeleton that's had a few clothes thrown over it. You look so sad a lot of the time. But I have to say your expression seems to lift once you start to speak. You even shine—like a lantern."

"Slavery is a fundamental ill, or more, it's an injustice."

Now Walt became aware of Chuck's presence: "I thought we'd cut that passage a long time ago." And, facing Lincoln: "The black people's March on Washington, three years ago now, do you approve of that? Is that what you want? Was that what you had in mind when you abolished slavery?"

At this point there is a gap in the recording—while Amen was turning the tape over. At the beginning of the B side, the technician apolo-
gizes for Lincoln's transgression: "I promise to look into it. Maybe it was
one of our guys' idea of a joke." He took a breath. "Sir?"

"Chuck?"

"I ... by mistake ... I happened to overhear you say you might have
enemies?"

"I don't remember saying that. You must have misheard."

"I must have misheard."

"You can leave me alone again now, thank you very much."

Amen retreated once more.

"When we created you and brought you to New York, to the World's
Fair, Mr. President, two years ago," Walt sat down again on the chair next
to the throne, "when you occasionally hurt people with your outbursts,
then one of my men turned to me and said: 'Do you think God might be
angry with us, Walt, for making a man in His image?'"

At that moment Abraham Lincoln got to his feet, and spoke fluently:
"May any American, any freedom-loving American, swear by the blood
of the revolution never to break the laws of our country ..."

"Perfectly fine. What else?"

"... May freedom become the political religion of our nation. Young
and old, rich and poor, all races, creeds and peoples should offer continual sacrifice at the altars of freedom ..."

"And where, in your opinion, is all this freedom going to lead? Our
youngsters grow their hair long, their beards hang down to their chests,
they play the ugliest, basest, most uncivilized jungle music. They swallow
mind-altering pills, take drugs like lunatics, fornicate like rabbits. It's all
going to end very badly, this fucking around, if you'll forgive the expression, I know you're not the child of sadness. It's going to end very badly.
Are you surprised that the son of a socialist—you must know my father
was a socialist to the marrow—could move so far to the right? There's a
simple explanation: When my men went on strike in 1941, I became com-

pletely disillusioned. It was so unjustified, so crass and disgusting, it turned my friends into enemies, my most gifted men became Communist mouthpieces, happy to repeat whatever the unionists vomited forth. Since then I've treated everything socialist or left wing as if it were the Black Death."

"When the war began"—curiously, the doll waited for Walt to finish— "three years ago now, neither one side nor the other, no one would have thought it possible it would still be going on today ..."

"I disagree again, Mr. President. After our victory in Southeast Asia, the evil regime in the Soviet Union is doomed to collapse. Then our GIs will walk through a liberated Moscow with machine guns. The people will rise up to welcome us. Red Square will be renamed after you, Mr. Lincoln, Marx Prospect after me ..."

Now the president and Walt both spoke at the same time, it is hard to make any sense of the voices, up to that point where Abraham Lincoln suddenly began to creak, to rattle and whistle, and collapsed on the stage. The doll fell on its front, held its mouth open, and babbled on: "The child has reached man's age, it has attained middle age, grown old and died. Now a whole nation is grieving for this man. Now a whole nation is grieving for this man. Now a whole nation is grieving for this man ... For this man ... Now a whole nation is grieving for this man ... For this man ... For this man ... Now a whole nation is grieving for this man ..." The voice grew lower and lower, the words lengthened, grew slower and thick until they finally ceased.

"Humpty Dumpty sat on a wall," recited Walt. "Humpty Dumpty had a great fall. All the king's horses and all the king's men couldn't put Humpty together again!"

Amen helped him in an attempt to resurrect Abraham Lincoln, born on February 12, 1809 in Hodgenville, Kentucky, shot on April 14, 1865 in a theater box in Washington, D.C. The total weight of the rubber, wood, wire and metal doll came to about one hundred and thirty pounds. No sooner had the two men successfully lifted Lincoln up than he seemed to be cured of his infirmity. He moved in the manner expected of him, spoke his lines flawlessly: "Our reliance is in the love of liberty which God has planted in our bosoms. Our defense is in the preservation of the spirit which prizes liberty as the heritage of all men, in all lands, everywhere. Destroy this spirit, and you have planted the seeds of despotism around your own doors."

"Are those the lines Lincoln normally speaks, Amen?"

"Of course, sir, Walt, always."

"The pillars of the temple of freedom are threatening to collapse," the sixteenth president of the United States intoned solemnly, "unless we, the heirs of the founding fathers of our nation, can succeed in replacing them by new pillars, hewn from the quarry of solid sense."

"Will you call a meeting for tomorrow morning. I want all those responsible for Lincoln to be present. No absentees. I don't like what I'm hearing."

"But sir, there haven't been any changes in two years now ..."

"In that case ... it's me who's changed. And stop calling me sir."

"Sorry."

"Call me Walt. Just Walt."

"I'm sorry, Walt."

"As we are facing a new predicament," the robot proceeded, "we need to learn fresh ways of thought. We need to cut free of the past, only then can our country be saved. Only then ... Can ... Our country ... Be saved. Saved. Saved."

"Much as I revere you, Mr. President," responded Walt, "your views no longer tally with mine. Evidently I've moved on, even in the last couple of years. A man changes in the course of his life."

"Divine Providence! ... Slave in Kentucky ... A furious struggle broke out ... Struggle, struggle, struggle broke out," the doll gave back. "The Egypt of the Pharaohs was smitten with ten scourges. Pharaoh's armies were drowned in the Red Sea, in their pursuit of a people that had served them for more than four hundred years. Divine Providence ..."

At this point on the tape there is the unmistakable sound of a large object striking against human flesh. That's followed by a couple of short screams—both from Walt. Chuck described to me later what happened. Abraham Lincoln's arms started flailing violently, turning into swinging clubs raining down blows on their creator, like the cudgel in the sack in Grimm's fairy tale of *The Magic Table.*

"Watch out, sir, oh my God!" cried Amen.

"The shepherd drives the wolf away from the throat of his flock . . ."

"Hit the main switch!" Walt yelled.

"All the armies of Europe, Asia, and Africa combined . . ."

"Hurry, Chuck, the power!"

". . . in a trial of a thousand years . . . !"

"Careful, sir!"

"Turn that goddamned power off!"

Backstage, Amen was fumbling desperately for the main switch, which under normal circumstances he would have had no trouble finding.

"Shall we expect some trans-Atlantic military giant to step across the ocean," intoned the president doll, still lashing out in all directions, "and crush us at a blow? Never! And crush us at a blow? Never! Never! Never!"

"Hurry, Amen!"

"All the armies of Europe, Asia, and Africa combined, could not by force, take a drink from the Ohio, or make a track on the Blue Ridge, in a trial of a thousand years. At what point then, is the approach of danger to be expected?"

In the few seconds remaining before Chuck finally found the switch and turned it off, the robot let go of Walt, and trotted backward in the direction of his chair of state. Sat down so hard that it splintered under him.

There was soft groaning to be heard from Walt. It was completely dark in the room now. He picked himself up, dusted himself off, secretly hoping his employee hadn't noticed that he'd been thrown to the ground in the course of the attack.

His chief technician bumped into corners, pillars, metal struts. He managed to grab his tape recorder from under the stage.

"At tomorrow's meeting," Walt said gruffly into the darkness, "we're going to announce that Lincoln will be withdrawn until further notice."

"Hold on, Walt, sir, I'll be with you in a moment, I always have trouble in the dark. I always go to sleep with the lights on, you see."

"Yeah ... I can understand that."

"Really, Walt? That makes me ... so pleased ..."

It took a while longer before they got to the front door, and found themselves out on Main Street again.

Chuck opened the passenger door of the limousine. It was almost midnight.

Walt took another swig from his flask. He motioned Chuck away, he had no desire to spend the next hour on the road only to arrive at an empty villa. He pointed his chin in the direction of the nearby building where he had his apartment.

In parting, he added: "You know, it's not just the technical difficulties that make me withdraw Abe Lincoln, Chuck."

"He's such an attraction ..."

They shook hands.

And after a pause, Walt said, in a low voice: "One more thing, Chuck."

Chuck pricked up his ears, like a beast smelling danger.

"You've got to lose some weight. You're too fat."

"I know, sir, Walt."

"You must be thirty or forty pounds overweight, at least. Lose it, will you!"

"Yessir, Walt!"

Amen settled behind the wheel of the Cadillac, in which, on this one night, he was being allowed to drive himself home. The door was still open.

"You know, Amen," Walt rested his hand on the roof of the car, "right up to his death, my father believed in the victory of the proletariat over capitalism. Every week he read the Socialist paper, *Appeal to Reason.* That was one more way I let him down . . . my father . . . Elias Disney . . ."

"Good night, sir."

"See you in the morning, Chuck."

And Disney turned away, moving languidly, with a slight limp, in the direction of the small brick fire station that matched the fire station in Marceline in every detail. On the first floor his red plush doll's house apartment was waiting for him.

CHAPTER FOUR

When I find myself lying awake at night, my first thought is always of him. I often lie awake, ever since the time he walked into my office and told me I'd been fired. Sometimes I'll spend an hour staring into the blackness, looking into the void, sometimes as much as two or three hours, before I can get to sleep again. I assail my thoughts with sentences we've spoken, with situations we've found ourselves in, with answers I didn't have the guts to give, from the time I was working for him, and from the time I was no longer working for him. I look back on the story of his life, as if it was closer and more familiar to me than my own. Even today, thirty years after our last meeting, it's him I think of the moment I wake up in the morning, and when I've put myself to bed at night.

A few weeks ago, when I first thought of finding a form for what I'd been through, I didn't know whether it should become a pamphlet of lamentations and accusations, a charade, or a heroic epic. I would try, and that was all I knew, to give an account of what had happened to me since my nineteenth year and our first meeting.

I was born in Vienna on October 9, 1936. My father, Egon Philipp Dantine, having worked in the garment business after he left school, took over a shirt factory in the Tirol in 1929. As a boy, it had been his dream to be a concert violinist, something his mother had also wanted for him, though his father wouldn't hear of it. I had to learn the violin as a boy, but to my parents' disappointment I never got very far with it.

My mother, Mathilde Juhasz, was an actress. Her parents came from Hungary, and around the turn of the century had settled in the Viennese suburb of Inzersdorf, where my mother was born. In the early thirties she had a considerable reputation, appearing with the likes of Käthe Gold and Paula Wessely, playing Shakespeare, Chekhov, Hauptmann, Ibsen, Strindberg. Some of the Austrian theater critics between the wars recognized my mother as one of the actresses audiences liked best. My sister, Marika, twelve years older than me, stayed behind in Austria with our grandparents, Mathilde's parents, when mother, father, and I emigrated to America. After the war, I rather lost contact with her, seeing her not more than four or five times in Vienna, on Lake Grundl, and in Los Angeles. She died a short time ago.

We started off living in Boston in the summer of 1938. After a year and a half there, we moved to Los Angeles, where Father was soon able to set up his own business, Phil's Dry Cleaners, which became so successful that he opened a chain of stores throughout Southern California. My mother's career unfortunately didn't survive our arrival in the United States—something she was always to remain bitter about. She did once play a European flower girl in a 1943 movie starring Edward G. Robinson, in which she had two lines: "Roses! Beautiful red roses!" and, as she was to emphasize to the moment of her death, was given "two close-ups!" but that was really the one exception. She did put on various German language poetry readings in Pasadena, Glendale, and Palm Springs, but that sort of thing couldn't have satisfied her. I remain convinced that her untimely illness was connected with the loss of her professional opportunities. Her life had remained thoroughly unfulfilled, or at least that's how it appears to me, looking back on it.

I was always told my artistic gift showed itself precociously. At the age of five, I could draw with perspective, and I did draw, every day, caricatures of my parents, babysitters, teachers, playmates in kindergarten, and, later on, my friends at school. One of my more successful works of the period, I still have it today, is of the open trunk of our cherry red Oldsmobile, all stuffed full of bags and household things. Father had bought a little house in Laguna Beach, halfway between Los Angeles and San Diego, and I can remember that even at the age of six or seven I used to do little watercolor sketches of the sand, the rocks, the little house, the Pacific breakers, and the hills all round.

I was a voracious reader. As I had a bilingual upbringing, I was able to read those works of German exiled literature to which my father was especially attached. But of all the novels I read when I was growing up, there was only one I was passionate about, and that was *Doctor Faustus* by Thomas Mann.

No sooner had I finished high school than—like my idol, Doctor Faustus's protagonist Adrian Leverkuhn, who felt himself born to compose—I meant to find work painting and drawing. I was dead set against studying. Father did what he could to talk me out of it. But the more he impressed upon me the necessity to go to college, the more I gravitated to being an artist. From a supermarket in North Hollywood, I received a commission to make an advertising film. It was my mother—she knew the manager—who got me the assignment. And even though I'd never attempted anything of the kind, I managed with a borrowed camera to make a short cartoon film. No one, I should like to emphasize, no one gave me any help. The result, a kind of fantastic dance of the various vegetables, fruits and meats, breads and cakes, and mineral waters, was so successful that other companies came to me with orders for similar films for their products.

I was just nineteen when I presented myself at the Burbank Studios on South Buena Vista Street, on the corner of Alameda. In the fall of 1955 a heat wave hit Southern California. For days on end the thermometer never dipped below one hundred in the shade. In the sunny rooms of the studio, however, thanks to an air-conditioning system that had been installed as far back as 1940, the temperature never rose above seventy, and you felt, the moment you set foot in the building, incredibly well.

I showed a portfolio of my most important sketches and watercolors, and brought along a couple of my cartoon films as well. The only reason I was applying for a job as cartoon draftsman was because father insisted that if I really didn't want to study, then I should at least use my talent for drawing in a way that brought in some money. The little promotional films wouldn't be sufficiently lucrative over time. I hadn't expected to get the job, but found myself hired on the spot. A film made in that studio, *Snow White* was the first film I had ever seen. Though I was just five and a half when I saw it with my mother on Sunset Strip in a little movie theater on the corner of Doheny Drive, I formed the impression then that everything was possible. Everything was doable. Every dream could become reality. The universe became my playground. I believed infinity lay at my feet.

Ward Kimball, one of the most daringly original animators to work for Disney, hired me in November 1955. When I inquired about Walt, he gave me to understand that I was bound to run into him sooner or later. It was another three weeks before I first laid eyes on him. He seemed moody and grouchy, reacted sourly when I presented myself to him with the words: "It was one of your films that changed my life!" "I know. *Snow White*. Well, I've heard that before." And he went off down the corridor that smelled permanently of linoleum and fresh paint, without giving me a second look. That initial meeting gave me the mixture of feelings I still have decades later when I think of him: bliss and hostility, reverence, awe, and rage.

A few months after that, we were both standing in the lunch line at the studio canteen. He knew I had recently begun to work on the very first drafts for *Sleeping Beauty*. Abruptly, he turned to face me: "The source of all originality and creativity, Bill, is dissatisfaction." I thought those words were remarkable at the time—and they lodged in my brain like a kind of siren song.

My dismissal in 1959, four years after I was given a contract, remains the most profound shock of my life. I was twenty-three years old. I would be lying if I said that I feel it any less now, as I'm putting these words on paper, than I felt it at the moment Walt walked into my office, one eyebrow raised, one lowered, and told me I was fired. I spent a lot of time subsequently without satisfying work, and planning my revenge. It was to take me seven years to summon up the courage to put my plan into action.

Even on the morning of the fateful day, Walt had had the recurring dream that had been plaguing him for years, the dream of trudging through the snowy streets of Kansas City. At half past three in the morning, he dreamed, he got up. It was so cold, he had no sensation in his fingers or toes: every day, including Sundays, the nine-year-old who had recently moved there from Marceline, was charged with delivering the *Kansas City Star* before the sun came up. His father didn't pay him a cent for it. He scampered across the porches; he wasn't allowed to stay on the pavement and toss the newspapers in the direction of the door—each one had to be placed under the mat. That was what his father had insisted on. So that the newspapers were shielded from the wind and snow. Some of the drifts were up to his chin—and this not in his dream, but winter after winter, in fact. At last he reached Cliff Drive, where he could warm up for a moment in the heated stairwells of the apartment buildings. Sat down on the stairs and dropped off for a minute, not more than a minute. And then it reared its head, the panic fear he was to dream of until his dying day: his father would beat him, as he had done often enough before, if he learned that his youngest son had fallen asleep on his paper route, or if he got to hear that one of the subscribers had failed to get his paper that day. Elias beat him until he was sixteen years old.

On summer days, on the porches that Walt crossed to deliver the papers, there would sometimes be toys left out overnight by the children. For a few seconds, he would clutch teddy bears, toy trains and cars, and quietly would play with wooden blocks and rag dolls with tiny glass bead eyes hanging on threads. And then the sun would slowly rise. "But on winter days it was goddamned dark, and the sun wouldn't show until I was in class," I heard him say once to a group of animators, preparing a scene from *Sleeping Beauty* that was to take place at daybreak. "I often fell asleep during lessons. That's how tired I was from having to get up so goddamn early."

*

It was Sunday, October 9, 1966, when my older son Jonathan and I paid our call on Walt in Holmby Hills, at 335 Carolwood Drive. Lillian had gone to the supermarket, if I'm not mistaken. Burt, the butler, and Jenny, the Australian cleaner, both had the day off. The master of the house—as he liked best to do—was tinkering with his locomotive. He had a flashlight in one hand, and a pair of pliers in the other. I can still see him, in his short-sleeved Hawaiian shirt and his baggy gray polyester slacks. He was wearing his favorite cowboy boots and a blue and white striped golf cap. A humid, strikingly hot day, even so early in the morning. The air carried the typical Los Angeles scent, a mixture of orange blossoms, smog, and the salty warm sea breeze.

The locomotive, a Central Pacific No. 173 from 1881, scaled down in a ratio of 1:8, and the three cars it pulled had ground to a halt after derailing off the narrow tracks. He liked these mornings without Lillian; he still tried to make her think he wanted to spend all his days with her beside him, but that wasn't the case, that hadn't been the case for some time. In fact, he enjoyed being on his own, tinkering with his railway, which crossed the park-like grounds. When did he ever have any time for himself? On Sundays, if then. Only on Sundays and holidays; every other day he spent at the studio in Burbank.

"I'm not complaining," he liked to say, "on the contrary, there's no greater happiness than uninterrupted work. If you want to create your own world, you need to work at least sixteen hours out of twenty-four, if not more, many more. And I have created a world of my own. People often ask me: What's your secret—how do you get to be so successful? How can we realize our dreams? And what I tell them is: you've gotta work. Total commitment of course isn't enough by itself: self-confidence is the most important element of success."

The tracks of his miniature railway led across bridges and viaducts, through tunnels and underpasses, past lofty eucalyptus trees and a red barn that I recognized as the barn that Mrs. Murray had told me about in Marceline. It served as the repair shop and locomotive hangar, and it was where the main fuses for the whole circuit were located. There was also a miniature station, with a sign drawn by one of his favorite draftsmen, Ollie Johnston: *Holmby Hills*. Walt usually sat up on the locomotive, his Lilly Belle, and if he had visitors, then they would take their places behind him on the little coal tender, or on one of the passenger cars.

They quarreled almost every day, Lillian and Walt, over the Carolwood-Pacific Railroad. She didn't like her husband's little whimsical hobby from the start, nor was she softened when he gave the locomotive the name *Lilly Belle*; if anything it had the reverse effect. He had half a mile of tracks laid across the garden, undertook various bulldozings and landscapings that Lillian didn't approve of. Well, it won't last long, she thought, when, in spite of all her protests, he started riding his train round the garden. And then his pastime had lasted another twenty years. "You've got your park in Anaheim!" she complained after the opening of Disneyland, in the summer of 1955. "You can ride your train around there as much as you wish. Why do I have to deal with all the noise and the soot and the smoke, here, in my house?"

None of it was the least use.

With increasing delight, he planned infractions of the speed limit, collisions, derailments. Repairing his railroad was the best medicine for him, aside from the meetings with Hazel George in the laughing room. Even the insides of the cars were true to life. In the dining car there were newspapers on the little tables; if you looked through the windows, you could make out the minute headlines: "Tsar Alexander II Falls Victim to Socialist Revolutionary Assassination Plot." And little plates with sweet knives and forks, and lamb chops no bigger than postage stamps, and green beans like matchsticks. And tiny little glasses and bottles, and miniature champagne corks!

Not that champagne was his favorite drink; whiskey was. He enjoyed its soft, smoky, sometimes scorching rush, and I'm convinced he drank more whiskey than any other alcohol in his later years. Irish, Scotch, Canadian, American whiskey, he didn't really mind, he just needed to feel that sweet bite on his gums and tongue, and that burning in his throat to help him regain his even temper. He had his first drink after he left his home at sixteen. He got a job as a vendor, selling coffee, sandwiches, and soda pop on the Santa Fe Express, eight hours each way; he worked sixteen hours a day on the Kansas City–Chicago run. "There's nothing like that blissful, heart-opening feeling of freedom that you get on a moving train!" he told a reporter from the Japanese newspaper *Yomyuri Shimbun* six months before he died. "And since the line led straight past Marceline, I could always look out the windows as we passed it, to see the houses, the pastures, the hills. Sometimes I had the feeling I recognized a certain dog I'd known there, or a cow, an ox, or a sow, all from the train as it went thundering on its way. One time, it must have been in 1917, I felt so homesick that I got off at Marceline, spent the night at my friend Clem Flickinger's house, and traveled on the next day. Of course, that almost cost me my job. Sometimes, I went on different routes, once I got as far as Pueblo, Colorado, and spent the night in a squalid little hotel there, and went back to Kansas City the following day. The floors were crooked, there was a stink of old food, cockroaches scuttled along the walls, mice crept out from under the floorboards, and I felt happier than at any time since my earliest childhood."

In one of these railroad hotels, my guess is that it was as much a brothel as a hotel, he had his first taste of whiskey. No one noticed that he stole it from the chef on the Santa Fe Express, who always used to carry a flask. And he smoked his first cigarette on one of these trips, on the toilet. His love of smoking goes back to those days, and was to be with him for the rest of his life. Not until 1964 did the United States Surgeon General begin publishing the warning: it was now almost certain—people had suspected it for a long time—that there was a connection between smoking and lung cancer. Walt Disney's favorite brand was unfiltered Lucky Strikes. He smoked those for decades, and in the last years of his life he took up French Gitanes, also unfiltered, one after the other, one after the other. "I never knew anyone to leave as many scorch marks on the furniture and the carpets and his clothes as my husband did," Lillian would often complain.

Of course, the illness that would kill him was connected to his chain-smoking, even if he did insist, to his last breath, to Hazel George anyway, that it was my sudden appearance, on October 9, 1966, that was the principal cause of his rapid decline. "Bill turned up like a cat," he said several times. "Oh, how I hate cats! The creeping, sneaky way they have of suddenly standing in front of you. Their disloyalty and hypocrisy. He took years off my life."

Walt thought he had just managed to correct the steering of his locomotive. And then there we were, standing in front of him all of a sudden, Jonathan, then nine years old, and me. Shortly after sunrise, we'd climbed over several fences separating the property from the street, and that to begin with had looked insurmountable to us. But then everything passed off surprisingly easily. I couldn't understand why there was no alarm system of the kind that had already been installed in places like Hollywood, Beverly Hills, Bel Air. Admittedly, if there had been an alarm, I would have been prepared for it. I'd read about how you detect the presence of one, and how to disarm it. In the days leading up to our ambush, I made certain that the property was not patrolled by a security guard. I walked up and down outside the house, under the ancient palms, even poked in the trash cans left at the end of the drive. Went through the

Disneys' garbage, unfortunately encountered nothing of interest, aside from innumerable and practically indistinguishable fan letters.

We had been observing Walt for quite a while, behind trees and bushes, on the edge of the vast, pale-blue swimming pool, watched him repair his Central Pacific, also overheard him talking to himself. We waited for Lillian to get the car out of the garage and drive away. My son had fits of laughter, and I thought we'd be discovered before we could accomplish anything. In my fear and annoyance, I reached out and smacked Jonathan. The sound of my hand striking his cheek must have been louder than his suppressed giggling.

I told my wife that Jon and I were taking a trip to the Mojave Desert. She was probably surprised that I didn't want to spend that particular Sunday with her, but she raised no objection. Even today, my son talks about this adventure of ours as a high point of his life. He was altogether more excited than I had imagined he would be in the weeks preceding our coup. In fact, both of us were terribly worked up. Our hearts were in our mouths. We could hardly believe that we had come so close to this idol, this celebrity of celebrities. Looking back on it, I find it hard to understand how I ever summoned up the courage that day to put my plan into effect, especially since only a month before, in Marceline, I had run away at the very last moment. My decision not to act on my own, but together with my son, doesn't seem to me now to have been such a great idea. Though Jonathan, at the age of thirty-nine, still raves about the experience, I think it was wrong to have taken him. He has yet to find the life he wants. He spent years going from state to state in his mobile home, looking for the right place to settle down. It must be at least partly the consequence of his less than perfect childhood, for which I am considerably to blame.

I was carrying a backpack, from which a faint squeaking came that only I could hear. It came from a mouse I had packed in a little wooden cage. (I had the same backpack with me in Marceline, with the same contents, and kept it in the trunk of my car. I found the mouse had suffocated when I pulled over near Kansas City to get some gas and study my maps.)

My hair was long and uncombed and greasy. I had stopped shaving since my return from Missouri and had a half-inch beard. My motley clothes looked as though I'd stolen them from the Pied Piper of Hamelin. Walt had instructed his staff in Anaheim: no long-haired men were to be admitted to Disneyland. But it became harder and harder to obey his order, the more numerous we flower children became, the more of us wished to visit the Magic Kingdom stoned out of our minds. Every day dozens of young men were turned away—refused admission on account of their hair length. Nor were any of his employees allowed to grow a beard, not even a mustache like the one Walt himself sported. And now one of that species turned up in his very house! I was jubilant, planned to write up my prank in the hippie and yippie papers and the counter-culture magazines. I could see myself becoming a hero of the Underground movement.

Jonathan bent down beside the cars, peered fascinatedly in at the windows, instead of keeping to our agreement. We had arranged that he was to confront our victim by hurling at him the words: "You robbed my childhood of its innocence!" Instead, there he was, stroking the derailed locomotive as if it were a wounded pet, while I was hopping from one foot to the other like a worried child. "You robbed . . ." I prompted Jonathan. And again: "my childhood . . . You robbed my child-hood . . ." Nothing.

Walt seemed neither surprised nor annoyed by our showing up in his garden. Instead he asked me for help: "You're just in time. Here, lend me a hand, will you!" He motioned to me to pick up the front end of the locomotive. At the same time, he lifted up the back. I was so astonished, I did what he said. And, thanks to my strength, because in those days I had broad shoulders and firm, strong arms, though I've since gotten flabby, we managed without much trouble to hoist the locomotive back on to the tracks.

Did he know who I was? After all, he hadn't recognized me once on the various occasions I stood in front of him in recent years. Or had he?

He sat down astride the locomotive, sounded a shrill whistle, thick clouds of steam billowed up, and the machine, without moving an inch, panted and hissed. Not a remarkable experience, I admit, but one that burned itself into my memory forever.

"So it wasn't the goddamned quadruplex valve after all," he swore. And did he ever swear! The words *shit* and *ass* and *damn* and *darn* spilled easily from his lips. (On the other hand, when he heard one of his animators call Mickey Mouse a four-letter word once, he fired the man on the spot.) Walt's nasal voice, which had echoed in my head ever since our parting, his Missouri twang, as he described it, I heard again for the first time in seven years, with the difference that now he was addressing me personally.

"Maybe . . . a spot . . ." I stammered, "a spot of oil . . . would help?"

At that, he turned to face me properly for the first time: "Aren't you a bit old to be running around like that? How old are you now? Late twenties? Older? Is that the new fashion? To barge in uninvited on private property?"

To which my son replied: "You're a lot older than my Daddy, and you're still playing with trains."

"Jonathan knows practically every single film from your studio." I sounded strangely proud.

"So, to what do I owe the honor of your visit?" He forced himself to remain calm.

"Today's my thirtieth birthday, Walt. Ever since the day you fired me, I've been planning this. Well, now I'm here."

"To assassinate me!" he joked.

"Hold on, hold on . . ." I remained astoundingly calm. "One thing at a time . . ."

He coughed. Earlier, long before his smoker's cough became so pronounced, we always knew: Here comes Walt! Because we could hear him clearing his throat as he came down the corridor to see how we were all getting on with whatever project we were working on. It was like an early warning signal for us to break off private conversations, or, for some of my colleagues, to put away work that didn't have anything to do with the studio. If we heard a cough, we knew: The boss is coming!

"One of your films changed my life," I picked up again, when his coughing finally subsided.

"Yes, Bill, I know, you've told me often enough. You came to America as a kid, with your parents. And *Snow White* was the first film you ever saw." He paused, drew a deep breath. "You know, your talent was obvious from every one of the drawings in your portfolio. You *begged* us to take you on. That wasn't necessary, I had already decided: I wanted Wilhelm Dantine to work on the preparations for *Sleeping Beauty*. We were always on the lookout for gifted draftsmen, even when my studio had a staff of a thousand. Whenever someone struck me as unusually talented, I gave him a chance. The only ones to suffer were those who no longer produced the work I expected of them. Those were the ones I had to let go."

"It was Ward Kimball who took me on. I didn't even meet you until weeks after that."

He laughed, laughed heartily. "You really think so, don't you? That Ward took you on? Not one decision was made without my say-so. He showed me your work. I hired you. Not him."

"*Snow White* was the first film I saw, too," my son called out, choosing the worst possible moment to remind us of his presence. I was truly surprised to hear that Walt himself had hired me. Or was he lying? On the other hand, how well he seemed to remember me.

"Daddy took me to see *Snow White* when I was just five years old," Jonathan went on, "and I got so excited I wet my pants."

"You weren't the only one, son. Theater owners all over the country wrote in to complain to me when the film came out. They had to get all their seats reupholstered. They were all reeking of piss."

I sat down on the lawn, and slipped off my backpack.

"Get up!" He raised his voice for the first time. "I'll meet you in the studio any time if you want to talk over the past. But would you be so kind as to leave my property right now." He reached into his pocket (he always had something to snack on), and came up with a handful of nuts and biscuit crumbs that he tossed into his mouth. From the vehemence of the hand movement, I could tell he was rather nervous.

I was pleased. "I like you better this way: a little outburst, that's what I'm used to from you. Less of that soft soap."

Jonathan picked up a rock, and aimed it at a robin.

"I'll see you out," Walt went on.

My son threw his rock. It just missed.

I stayed where I was, cross-legged on the lawn. "You never gave me a single word of praise." I was annoyed at how small my voice sounded, but my anxiety was making it hard for me to breathe. "Only slogans like: 'Let's bomb the shit out of the Russians!' or 'The Soviet Union is evil incarnate!' 'Let's send in our G.I.'s to capture the Kremlin!' But something like: 'Wilhelm, or Bill, if you'd rather, those drafts you did yesterday, the three fairies and their cloaks, that cute little owl and her amazing cape-dance, your Prince Philip on his proud charger, you are so gifted, just go on as you are!' Never happened. Never occurred to you. You were a sphinx. Never came up to me and asked: 'Who are you? Where are you from? What's on your mind?'"

I didn't know then how carefully he investigated the backgrounds of every one of his employees, without our knowledge. I had no idea how incapacitated he was by bouts of deep depression that recurred throughout his life.

"If I could have it my way," he replied, "I'd have one vast machine built that would replace all of you sons of bitches."

"Kindly remember you're in the presence of a child," I admonished him, "and be a bit more careful how you express yourself."

"It doesn't bother me," called Jonathan. "That's the way you talk at home!"

Walt's patience was exhausted. He threatened to hand me over to his friend, the sheriff of Holmby Hills. He would report what had happened, trespassing on private property carried a severe penalty. In some states, California was one of them, it was permitted to shoot trespassers on sight, even without a warning.

"In the future, I'm going to have to wall myself in, like in a fort," he said to himself. And set off toward the gleaming white, faux-colonial villa, I imagined, to make a phone call. Then my son stood in his way, holding a slingshot with a wide elastic band—I had no idea he'd taken his little homemade toy weapon with him on our mission. That was the first moment Walt seemed to feel a twinge of fear.

"He's going to have to call for help," I crowed, "the poor, defenseless little man. The King of America held at bay by a nine-year-old kid! Feeling scared, are you? I never saw the least sign of fear in your eye in the two or three minutes it took you to wreck my life, seven years ago! With your sly, ironic little smile. Well, in a word: I want satisfaction from you in any way you can give it, financially or otherwise. You could, for instance, add my name to the credits on *Sleeping Beauty*, before or after, it's up to you. My name first, followed by those of Frank Thomas and Eyvind Earle! Just a suggestion, to get your imagination going ..."

For him, who never allowed anyone to contradict him, to be put through something like this! He always thought there was something godlike about himself. I'm not exaggerating here. I'm just repeating the way he used to speak of himself, think of himself. "I'm hewn from the same rock as Thomas Edison and Henry Ford. I'm a son of this great country, a genius in the tradition of the greatest, wealthiest, most beautiful nation on the planet," is something he said to us more than once, and he wasn't being ironic then. "In Brazil"—I'd been working for him for a year when he came out with this—"for instance, in Rio, I'm more famous than Santa Claus."

This rather unimpressive, uncultivated nobody, a man who left school at fourteen and a half is known to children on all seven continents to the present day. And will remain known, well into the new millennium. From Japan to Mongolia, from Nepal to Portugal, from Greenland to Peru, billions of people know who Walt Disney is. That's the most hurtful thing of all as far as I'm concerned: that a man like Walt could achieve such lasting significance. The immeasurable gift that I, Wilhelm Dantine, possess, gets me nowhere. Whereas his lack of talent takes him to immortality. I was afraid then that it would rob me of my sanity.

When he was shown the centaur sequence from *Fantasia* for the first time, that wonderful explosion of illustrations created by Fred Moore, Ward Kimball, Art Babbitt, and sixteen other animators, set to the music of Ludwig van Beethoven's Sixth Symphony, the *Pastoral*, he turned to Mark Cooper, one of his assistants at the time, and remarked—and he can't have been joking, no, this is deadly earnest: "Wow! This is really going to put Beethoven on the map!"

He wasn't acquainted with the work of Gustav Mahler or Johannes Brahms, of Anton Bruckner or Claude Debussy. He didn't know the operas of Richard Wagner or Richard Strauss. He wasn't ashamed to say: "When I hear Bach, I can see a steaming bowl of spaghetti in front of me!" As soon as someone talked to him about literature, he made no bones about the fact that he had never heard of most books and their authors. He knew next to nothing about art history of the nineteenth and twentieth centuries. Cézanne and Matisse, Manet and Monet, Braque, Chagall, and Klee were blanks to him. He hadn't even heard of most of their names. Once I showed him an illustration from one of my art books, a reproduction of Goya's famous war painting, *Panic*. "I like the guy who did that! What's his name again?" was Walt's response. "Francisco de Goya," I replied. "Goya, eh? Well, he's good, your Goya!" he said. "Where's he live?" Then again, he was a friend of Salvador Dalí's, who spent months working on Walt's project, *Destino*, based on a Mexican ballad. I have seen the many drafts for ballerinas, baseball players, dancing bicycles, and singing beetles that Dalí drew in 1946. They are among his best works, and they all disappeared into the studio archives.

"Walt was a magician, my dear Mr. Dantine," Dalí was to explain to me in the late 1970s in a suite at the Hotel Meurice in Paris, in the presence of his wife Gala, who had smacked him across the face so hard that morning that I could still clearly see the red marks made by her fingers. "The Disney magic is innocence in action. He has the innocence and unself-consciousness of a child. He still looks at the world with uncontaminated wonder, and with all living things he has a terrific sympathy. Do you understand me, Mr. Dantine? He had an endless love for all living creatures, everything that creeps and crawls. It was the most natural thing in the world for him to imagine that squirrels and mice might have feelings just like his."

"I am folklore," the sly farmer's boy often recited to us. "I am apple pie and vanilla ice cream, popcorn, and the song on everyone's lips. I'm a proverb from Mother Goose that everyone's heard. Call me Father Goose. And Mickey is my prophet."

The most sensible thing for him to do would have been to leave me there without a reply, to go into his house and call Sheriff O'Connor. In all likelihood, if he'd done that, I would have given up. But instead, he stopped in front of me, drew himself up to his full height, stroked the thin gray-white mustache on which thick beads of sweat had formed, and made an effort to defend himself: "The very first thing you were told when you started working for me, even before you signed your contract, was: 'We're pleased you're coming to work for us. We will insist on your bearing in mind that *one* name and one name only is being sold here. Should you therefore hope to sell the name Wilhelm Dantine,' because that was what you still called yourself then before you restyled yourself as Bill, 'then you should quit on the spot!' Were you told that at the time, or weren't you?"

Jonathan replied on my behalf: "Papa always says you didn't even invent the mouse. Nor Donald either. Is that right? What about the Beagle Boys?"

It was clear that he felt like giving my fearless, long-haired kid a smack in the face or a kick in the pants—it was written all over him. But he remained motionless, stunned. I reminded him of a conversation we'd had two years after I'd joined the firm: "I was asking you how the mouse came to be invented. Do you remember what you told me then?"

He didn't speak.

"What you said was: 'Now Bill, in all honesty, I haven't got a clue how we hit upon it. We were looking for a new animal, sure, after that producer crook Mintz stole Oswald, my rabbit. I had always hated cats, although the very earliest cartoons had had cats in them. I wanted a little animal, so a mouse seemed a good idea. Kids like animals that are small and cute. In a way, I think we owed the idea to Charlie Chaplin. What we were trying to come up with was a charming little fellow who showed just a bit of Chaplin's melancholy as well ... a little critter that keeps trying to do its best. And doesn't always make it.' Do you remember saying that to me, Walt?"

Still he didn't speak.

"Do you remember saying that, my Daddy wants to know!" Jonathan backed me up.

"It's really not much like the official version, you know: you were on your way from New York to Los Angeles, in the sleeper car, after you'd lost Oswald the rabbit to Mintz, and you happened to remember a mouse you'd once given the name Mortimer, just as you were starting out on your career, when you were running a firm called Laugh-O-Grams, in Kansas City, and Mortimer was the tamest of the ten mice you kept in a cage, and the only one who was entitled to sit next to you on the drawing table and watch you draw. Not much like the story of how the rhythm of the train wheels went *Chug-chug-chug-chug-mouse-mouse-mouse-mouse-chug-chug-chug-chug*, nothing about how the shrill whistle—you can read this stuff in all the official accounts—seemed to go *A-m-m-mou-mouse!* all through the night, or how you got out at Los Angeles having decided to make a mouse named Mortimer the new hero of your company. And that it was at Lillian's insistence that Mortimer was changed into the gentler, kinder Mickey that very same day. No, you didn't give me a word of that whole fairy tale when I asked you about the origins of the mouse, your

'Walter Ego,' which went on to attain a comparable fame to Leonardo's *Mona Lisa* and Michelangelo's *David* and Van Gogh's *Sunflowers* . . ."

Walt's cheekbones were working. He looked livid.

"Working for you was the happiest time of my life, it was a privilege and an honor." I began pulling out of my backpack sketches and drawings that I had once made for him, both line drawings and large watercolors and gouaches that I kept all together in a cardboard cylinder. "To make something out of nothing, with teamwork, among a group of friends. My first sixty-eight drafts for *Sleeping Beauty*, here they are, you see, from the fairy robes to the dragon sequence at the end, from wicked Maleficent through to the angular rooms in the castle, see, all mine . . ."

"That belongs to *me*!" He coughed. "It's the property of my studio! You're nothing but a common thief," he berated me, coughing ever more violently. "How did you manage to get at . . . those drawings?"

"I picked them up over the Christmas break in 1959, because they are *my* property, Mr. Disney, not yours. And almost all of what I did for you then, ended up being used. Only, it's strange, my name never appears anywhere. It's always just your name, your signature that goes up in lights! Where are your collaborators credited, can you tell me that? Not on the silver screen, that's for sure. For forty years, you've been going around in the king's new clothes. Not *one* of the drawings that your films are based on, not a single one of them, is even by you. Not in any of the films. Even the technique of animation is beyond you. Every one of us who ever worked for you knew that. Of course, you knew how to get pictures to move. But the art of converting ideas into action, of charming living protagonists out of paper characters—all that has remained completely baffling to you. You never got it."

He pressed his hands over his ears.

My voice grew louder and louder, to reach him: ". . . and the thousands upon thousands of comic books, things are no better there: Uncle Scrooge? Gladstone Gander? Gyro Gearloose? The Three Nephews? Pluto? Goofy? Neither drawn by you nor even *conceived* by you. Just sporting your name, that's all. Carl Barks, a real genius, was responsible for everything in the magazines. And even now he goes on drawing, week after week, month after month, decade after decade! Every one of the Donald-and-his-three-nephews-plus-Uncle-Scrooge stories, whether they're caught up in some Viking story, or hunting the world's only remaining unicorn, way down in Tierra del Fuego, it's all come out of his head. And hardly anyone in the world has ever heard of Carl Barks. *You're* the thief, Walt."

"Never in all my life have I encountered such wickedness . . ."

"You never allowed your animators to get the fame they deserved. You pumped and pumped and pumped all the creative juices out of us, in order to represent our ideas and our achievements as your ideas and your achievements to the world! No sooner did someone come up with an idea, but within seconds you were claiming it as yours. Ub Iwerks, just to give a name to one more of these shadows of yours, did mountains of work for you. If it weren't for him, the goddamned rodent wouldn't even exist. In fact, I suspect that it was Iwerks who *invented* Mickey. He wasn't just the first to draw him, I think he made him up in the first place."

"Will you shut up now and let me get a word in, you freak! You *hippie!*"

"Not even your cute, round signature—and this certainly represents the single most revealing detail about your whole doubtful personality—not even your *signature* is your own! You had one of your best animators draw it for you. And then, ever since, for decades, you've had to try and fake it, but of course you never managed to do it right, your versions always looked ridiculous, diseased! And you went on to treat Fred Moore so appallingly badly that he drowned his sorrows in drink—in 1952, at the age of forty, in the prime of life, he drove his car into a tree."

"Never in all my life have I been subjected to such vile, baseless attacks, you nobody, you ridiculous creature," Walt Disney began his counter-attack. "Except once, when that little gaggle of my employees had the bright idea of getting a Commie-inspired strike going against me, and started agitating for a union of animators! Has anyone ever heard of anything so ludicrous? A cartoonists' union! They came to me and accused me of being a filthy rich exploiter, and at a time when Roy and I were up to our ears in debt to the Bank of America to the tune of several million dollars! Your father, a textile manufacturer if I remember correctly, always encouraged you to follow your dreams, you softy. To be an artist or whatever it was you wanted to be. Every door stood open to you. My father just threatened to beat me. And he didn't just threaten—he beat me for next to nothing. You grew up as a pampered only child, like your brattish son here, whom you saw fit to bring along. I had four siblings, and when I lit out on my own, I often didn't have the money to buy a can of beans. I couldn't pay to get my shoes repaired, so I ran around in busted shoes. I didn't have my own bathroom until I was twenty, I used to take showers at the YMCA, and all the time you were growing up you had a marble bathroom to yourself. I had thirty dollars in my pocket when I got to Hollywood in 1923. And then I made something of myself! A modern magician . . . !"

"An averagely successful American CEO is what you made of yourself," I butted in, "nothing more than that."

He launched himself at me!

I leaped aside, ran twenty feet or more, like a cat, frightened when its victim suddenly puts up fight. He chased after me, caught up with me. And slapped me, which did me a lot of good, strangely enough. I laughed out loud, called to Jonathan: "Are you watching, one day you'll be able to tell the world about the kind of guy nice old Uncle Walt really was . . ."

"What was that you just said, you degenerate freak?" It was only now that he really lost his temper. His voice cracked with indignation. Like the torero whose task is to provoke the bull into a blind rage before the final showdown, I had achieved my end. I had never seen him in a state like this. "Do I read you correctly? That all these films are supposedly not mine? That they're not by me? Beginning with the very first, *Oswald the Rabbit*, which that Jew Mintz stole from me under near-criminal circumstances. Oswald was my creation, through and through, only I didn't realize then that the damned distributor owns the rights! From *Alice in Cartoonland* and the seventy-five *Silly Symphonies*, from the first of the *Mickey* films and *The Three Little Pigs* and *Snow White* and *Pinocchio* right on down to the present day, and my very latest hits, like *Mary Poppins*: for forty years, every scene in every picture was inspired by me and steeped in me, my wishes and fantasies, my suggestions and changes. Don't I act out every single part, however tiny, right down to the crook of the little finger, before the animators get to work? Don't we always spend days and nights in the tiny room under the stairs, our so-called sweat box, talking through the things we have in production, putting in improvements, even sweeping changes? You know that, of course you do, you've been there often enough in your time with me. No *pencil stroke* is done without my say-so. Didn't I set up a special school for my artists at the end of the thirties? And drive them back and forth myself, to downtown LA or wherever it was they were living, because hardly any of them could afford a car in those days. I installed a little zoo in the studio, so that the new guys we took on would have the opportunity of observing animals in movement—rabbits, mice, a couple of deer, a goat, a cow, a monkey. You must know that, you saw it all when you joined. But for me, you would all have remained nobodies, every single one of you. Just like the ones who left me to go and work for someone else—they all ended up as nobodies, without exception! I am in no sense of the word a great artist, but when did I ever claim that? I always had men working for me whose skills were greater than my own. Anyone with the slightest interest in me must know that I was and am dependent on hundreds of other people. I am an ideas man. Or are you trying to deny that? Deny our daily story meetings, where the characters took shape? Every single one of them?" He broke off, struggled for breath. "Oh, what's the point!" He was wracked by another coughing fit.

Jonathan and I stood there, not knowing what to do with ourselves. He was listening attentively, much more so than when it was me or his teachers or some relatives talking to him. Now he gave me a signal that it was time for us to go.

"The only reason my daddy's so angry with you," to my horror, he seemed to be trying to soothe Walt, "was because you were so mean to him seven years ago, at Christmastime." And with that he walked away.

I called to him not to go, to stay and keep me company. The action, I shouted, was just about to begin.

He didn't listen to me, but disappeared into the far end of the garden, probably hoping I would come after him. I heard afterward that he waited for me for a long time by the fences, then, when I didn't come, went inside the magnificent villa, and gave himself a tour. He ran into fine paintings, saw a life-sized bust of Abraham Lincoln, found a glass-fronted cabinet that, he later told me, contained at least thirty golden Oscar figurines. He was struck by the enormous radiogram, which had been enclosed with a record player and a tape recorder in one broad cabinet of teak. The collection of records, he said, had been by far the largest he had ever seen. But the thing that impressed him most was a dark room at the back of the building, where he had just been able to make out a small cinema, its screen concealed behind heavy curtains. He saw the rows of seats and the projection room, but also a machine from which you could help yourself to Coca Cola and ice cream. I wanted to hear many more details from his reconnaissance, and badgered Jonathan for a long time afterward with my questions, but never succeeded in getting any more precise information out of him.

Walt clearly remembered the moment my son had referred to. I could see in his face that his thoughts had wandered back to the fall of 1959. *Sleeping Beauty*, embarked on in January of that year, proved a financial setback for the studio. The production had cost six million dollars. Of course he was looking for other people to blame than just himself to carry the responsibility for the looming debacle.

There was another thing: in September 1959, Nikita Khrushchev was paying an official state visit to the United States. In the course of it, the Soviet premier had also come to Hollywood, and, through intermediaries, had let it be known to Walt that he would very much appreciate a chance to see the Magic Kingdom in Anaheim. To go carooming down the Matterhorn on a sledge, to stand on the deck of the Mississippi steamer while audio-animatronics alligators emerged out of the yellow brown water, to get to know the park in all its myriad aspects, taking in the Cinderella castle and the evening parade, that would be the highlight of his visit to the U.S. For reasons that never became clear, though I assume today that J. Edgar Hoover and the F.B.I. were involved, the visit never came about, foiled by the State Department, ostensibly for security reasons. Khrushchev was outraged. He refused to accept that the trip could not take place. In the course of a press conference he claimed to journalists from all over the world that his request had been turned down because of some political machinations. Mark Timmerman and Sidney Frost easily convinced me—and me alone—to sign a memorandum they had immediately drawn up and would make available to the Soviet delegation in Los Angeles. In it, it said that Walt had knowingly and personally put a stop to the visit in order not to permit the first secretary of the Communist Party of the USSR to reap an international publicity coup. Because an afternoon spent amid the attractions of Frontierland and Fantasyland would certainly have played well with a public all over the world. (Although I wasn't a very political person, I did believe in the necessity for détente between the superpowers, and I did believe that signing the memorandum was the right thing to do.) Our letter was intercepted by Hoover's agents. And Walt, deeply offended, found it so low and reprehensible that he fired the three of us on the very day he read the document. Two of us, Frost and myself, were involved with the *Sleeping Beauty* fiasco as well. That would have made the decision even easier for him. He showed up at our little drawing desks, at the time we were sharing a single small office, busy with the first drafts for the *101 Dalmatians*. He stood in the doorway to our little cell, holding up our letter, and asked if we had written it. Didn't wait for us to reply (we were rather naïve and had no idea how it could ever have fallen into his hands), but in the same breath told us we were fired. I denied any part in it, claimed not to have initiated the thing, but he didn't want to hear another word, and turned his back on us.

"But what angered me most," he told me now, and I had a sense of the fear slowly melting away from his features, since my son had vanished, "was the fact that the truth of the matter was so very different. As a matter of fact, I was very much looking forward to Khrushchev's visit, and had prepared myself thoroughly for a meeting with him, read up on his life, read one of his speeches against Stalin. Of course I wanted to ask him some hard questions as well, sure I did, but he would have been up for that. And Lillian, who really wasn't interested in politicians and actors and royalty at all, not even Eisenhower or Kennedy or Johnson, she really wanted to meet Khrushchev. I had rarely seen her so excited. We were both looking forward to the moment when I would take the general secretary to the long row of ships in our underwater show, and say: 'And here, Nikita, is the eighth largest submarine fleet in the world!' So the goddamned cancellation was as much of a surprise and a disappointment for us as it must have been for you or Mr. Nikita Khrushchev, you can take my word on that. But then, you know, there was something else that really pissed me off, because it demonstrated that the Bolshevism in the ranks of my own staff had still not been rooted out. I had learned, and you may as well hear about this today when it no longer matters, that you had also been making efforts to whip up feeling against me in another context, namely the arrest and the conviction of Charles Spencer Chaplin; the House Un-American Activities Committee had asked me for a couple of pieces of information, yeah, sure, and I told them what I knew, namely that Chaplin had become a lousy Commie sympathizer. You and your pals in the studio, you turned that into a whole saga of Walt the wicked wolf persecuting the poor little lamb Charlie. And you had the gall to pass caricatures of me around, really ugly ones, real crude pieces of work, by the way. And that must have been why I fired you, Bill Dantine, at least as much as your totally fabricated claims about my role in the Khrushchev visit!"

"In terms of inspiration, you owe a greater debt to Charlie Chaplin than anyone else in the world," I retorted. "You ought to be ashamed of yourself for trying to wreck the life of that demigod. Next to him you're a sparrow to an eagle. There's a cosmic gulf, a chasm of emptiness, between you and Chaplin, both in human and artistic terms. And your slander was partly responsible for him being refused reentry into the States. Even the fact that you were willing to testify before McCarthy's committee deserves the most severe punishment, unless you apologize to him—it's never too late!"

He performed some curious rowing motions in the air: "Stop it, Bill! Enough already!"

But no, I wouldn't be reined in, not now: "You know, you ruined my life with one blow. Why should I stop, now that I've finally got you in my sights? I staggered from job to job, one temporary after another. Whatever I could get. I've had nothing but bad luck and disappointments, time after time. There's nothing more humiliating than feeling this desperate hunger and thirst to show your creativity, and not being able to satisfy it anywhere. You are personally responsible for the fact that nothing in my life has turned out well. And that's why I've come to see you today, Walt. I've made the decision ..."

I broke off.

For a while we both remained silent. His sunken cheeks looked creased. There were big bags under his eyes. Why didn't he run into his house at last, and phone for help?

"What ... what decision is that?" Every word cost him a huge effort.

I made no reply.

"You're drunk, Bill. Or stoned perhaps. Come on, go home now ... please, go. Your son's waiting for you. Don't leave him by himself."

"You know, Walt, in Marceline, not long ago, when the swimming pool was inaugurated ..."

"You were there. I know. I know it now. Of course I thought there was something familiar about you ..."

"If you'd talked to me then, in Marceline, instead of being all proud and aloof, maybe I'd have spared you my visit today."

"I was neither proud nor aloof. I felt incredibly well and happy there. Like I do every time I go to Marceline. That place is my Shangri-La. You know it is."

"You looked through me as if I wasn't there."

"You should have spoken to me. But now instead, you'll be going to prison. Was it worth it?"

"Absolutely. One hundred percent."

"Listen, you're going to be severely punished for this."

"And then there's my most important cause that in all the years of my being with you you've never once taken on board," I continued. "I must have come to you a dozen times with the idea, and I'm damned if I ever heard a syllable from you, just a grunt and a shake of your ugly head: I'm talking about my idea of making a film of *Hans in Luck*. What a magnificent, profound, and philosophically weighty story!"

"We're not in the philosophy business, Bill. We do entertainment."

"As if that Grimm's fairy tale wasn't entertaining! After seven years of working for his master, Hans is paid: a great, big lump of gold . . ."

"I'm familiar with the story."

"The lump of gold gets too heavy for him to carry, so he trades it for a horse."

"The horse throws him, so he swaps the horse for a cow."

"The cow kicks him, so he swaps the cow for a pig." As I spoke, I could envision each word as a picture, a scene, flowing in front of me, I saw the gold, the horse, the cow, the pig. "He loses the pig, he swaps it for a goose . . ."

Walt interrupted me: ". . . and so on and so forth, until by the end he's left with nothing, absolutely nothing, and he returns home to his mother with empty hands. So, what's entertaining about that? It might satisfy your warped brain, a lofty metaphor like that, but not my audience of billions."

"What about the hundreds of drawings you had me do for that 'Chaunteclere' project?"

"What 'Chaunteclere'? Remind me."

"Of course you forgot. Why wouldn't you, it was one of my ideas, after all. Which you liked, apparently, to begin with. Chaunteclere the cock, the champion singer. Based on Edmond Rostand's play of the same name. For six months, I supplied you with flawless sketches. And then all at once, it was: no, this isn't for us. I didn't even get to hear that one little word, 'sorry.'"

"'Chaunteclere' . . . yes, it does seem to ring a bell. It just wasn't right for us. End of story."

My head was spinning, all the complaints, accusations I'd carefully prepared for this moment were now swarming around my brain in confusion. "I heard your name's on the final list for this year's Nobel Peace Prize." I shouted. "*You* of all people, Walt? What a laugh! You, who not only told us you thought the extermination of the Indians was justified, but described it as a healthy necessity, a cleansing for our nation. You, who taught us that Indians were wild, bloodthirsty savages, who had to be wiped out. One of the most horrific genocides in the history of mankind—justified and highly praised by Mr. Walt Disney! You're to get the Peace Prize? Walt Disney, a great humanist! A second Albert Schweitzer! You, who were proud of your reception by Benito Mussolini in his pomp, in the marble halls of his dictator's citadel in Rome. You, who refuse to have a single black working for you in your studio. Who's against the integration of blacks into society, now that it's finally begun! And—this has less to do with world peace, but I have to tell you just the same—you, who never allowed one single woman to take part in the creative process! Women are good for copying and painting and coloring in a man's sketches and blueprints and ideas, but never may they provide the least creative impetus! You even parked the 'in-betweeners' in a separate building, to prevent any encounters between the ladies and the gentlemen . . . ! And if a woman happened to be caught in the men's building, she was fired on the spot."

He should have known that it was a waste of time trying to use calm language and sensible arguments with me. Now, instead of finally breaking off the conversation, he committed the foolish mistake of egging me on still more: "That's just so typical of you Jews—sitting in judgment on others. The gall it takes! Would a Christian ever talk to me like this? You think you're always in the right. And that we're always in the wrong. Why is it you keep having to raise yourselves above the Gentiles, and show them that you're better, nobler, juster men than they are? Is that never going to end? Hasn't history taught you enough of a lesson yet?"

"I am a Gentile, Walt." I could now hear the mouse squeaking very loudly, and it cut me in my belly, my back, my chest. I undid my backpack, started burrowing in it, and immediately forgot what it was I'd meant to look for.

"I always thought . . . " he was flustered and awkward, "I always took you to be . . . one of the few Jews . . . I had in my employ . . . I don't get it—so what did your folks *leave* for . . . ?"

"Because after the Nazis took over, in March 1938, they couldn't stand it in Austria any more, that's why, sir. Because they felt solidarity with their friends, who, overnight, became victims of persecution. Among them there were painters, architects, musicians, writers. For instance, my mother was a close acquaintance of Felix Salten, who had to flee Vienna, as you are probably unaware, as you seem to be unaware of most things about Salten, other than the fact that he provided you with the original story of *Bambi*. It's rare enough for you to get so excited about a book. 'A Story of Life in the Woods,' as the subtitle has it. Years later, you had another one of his stories filmed, *Perri*, the story of a heroic squirrel. I happened to be in the room when you took on the director. This time it wasn't an animation film, but a feature film, shot in the wilds of Wyoming and Utah. Salten supplied you with the original source to a third screenplay as well, *The Dog from Florence*, which became *The Shaggy Dog*, which you produced at the end of the Fifties. Felix Salten a Jew? You probably had no idea. Am I right? And that he was the author of one of

the greatest and steamiest pornographic novels ever written, I'm refer-
ring to the story of Josefine Mutzenbacher? No? No idea? Just as well,
because if you had known, you'd never have made *Bambi*, that's for sure!
I know the first sentences of the Mutzenbacher book by heart. Would
you like me to recite them for you?"

"Please don't . . ."

"I became a whore at an early age, I have experienced everything a
woman can . . ."

"That's enough . . ."

". . . everything a woman can experience in bed, on tables, chairs,
benches, propped against bare walls, lying in the grass, in dark alleyways,
in trains, and barracks, and prisons, and I don't regret any of it . . ."

He buried his head in his bony hands, massaged his brow with his
fingertips.

"As I say: Vienna, 1938. I don't know if you're capable of putting yourself in the position of people who are declared outlaws overnight, and
are driven into death. But maybe this is the first time anyone has told
you about these things."

He knew about the death camps, sure he did. He was familiar with the
course the war had taken in Europe, but he couldn't stand to hear such
stories. On the other hand, in 1955, the California chapter of the B'nai Brith
gave him their highest award, for his life's work. To his way of thinking,
it was a waste of time "digging up" these as he called them "sad events"
twenty years after they had occurred. As early as the mid-fifties, he
thought of them as obsolete, as "over."

At first he didn't notice that I had now spread out the entire contents
of my backpack on his lawn: paints, brushes, razor blades, a thick piece
of rope, and the mouse lying panting for air in its tiny wooden cage—all
laid out in a row. I called for my son several times, but he seemed to have
disappeared for good.

"What's all this stuff?" Walt finally asked. It felt as though minutes had
passed.

After that, everything happened very quickly: first I rolled around on a carpet of three or four of my large-format sketches (I didn't pull out any more than that, and I tried to choose what seemed to me the least valuable of my drawings). I felt like a dog, wildly rubbing my back on the grass, my arms and legs in the air. Then suddenly I leapt up, and started slashing open my cheeks with one of the razor blades. Smeared the blood, which came gushing forth, on to the locomotive, then all over my face, dipped the paintbrush in the pots of color. I daubed myself from head to foot in red, blue, yellow, and green, until my clothes started to feel damp and chill. The whole time, I didn't say one word. Puffing and groaning accompanied my every movement. I felt full of strength, capable of uprooting trees, fences, statues.

Walt shouted at me, "Stop this crazy nonsense immediately!" I advanced, quivering, bleeding, trembling, ripped off my wet shirt, and then my dripping trousers, stood in front of him in my shorts, daubed in color from top to toe, and finally looped the rope around my neck. He was afraid, as I later heard, that I was about to climb the nearest tree and hang myself before his eyes.

And then I yelled: "I curse you."

Those three words, nothing more. I carried on with my twitching St. Vitus dance, twirling the rope through the air like a lasso. I knew that the one thing he couldn't stand was the sight of blood. There wasn't a drop of blood in any of his films, not in the animated ones or in any of the wildlife documentaries or features. So I pulled down my shorts, and sliced a wound in my right upper thigh, which immediately started to bleed profusely. The wounds on my cheeks were gushing now. I had an erection, it seemed to stick out half sideways. It was as though I'd never noticed that crookedness in my penis before. From that moment on, Walt kept his eyes on the ground.

I think he probably didn't catch the last act of my visitation, at any rate he failed to refer to it in any of his subsequent accounts. With my Swiss army knife, I slaughtered the mouse (it was half-dead anyway), shuddered at the hideous release of its bodily fluids, felt the dying mass as a sort of cross between lava and vomit, and yawed between nausea and euphoria.

At first I wasn't aware that Walt had left the garden. It wasn't until I heard Jonathan whisper "Daddy!" to me, that I started to come to my senses. I turned around, my son let it be known to me that Walt was calling the police. He handed me my pants and shirt, helped me pick up all that was lying around as quickly as he could.

We heard Walt give his name and address. We ran for the gates and fences that we had scaled hours before, and made it back to the car without injury and without any particular trouble.

*

He came out into the garden again. Neither the sketches nor the pots of paint, neither the items of clothing nor the rope and the brushes were anywhere to be seen. In spite of the panic rush, Jonathan and I had even managed to pick up the mouse cadaver and its little wooden cage, and stuff them back in the backpack.

What followed I had related to me several times by Hazel George, going on what Walt told her two days after my visit. The first thing he did was to search the grass for signs of my action. He was unable to find a single drop of blood or paint. There was a dark smear on the side of the locomotive, but that turned out to be machine oil. He sank to his knees, and then stretched out on his belly on the grass. The tall wrought-iron gates opened, and Lillian drove up in her white Pontiac, the crunch of the gravel in the driveway seemed to go right through Walt.

She saw her husband sprawled on the lawn. Her first thought was that something might have happened to him in the course of one of his de-railments. She knelt down beside him, touched him for the first time in weeks, and saw how pale he looked. What most worried her was the fact that he was lying on his stomach and not on his back.

"What happened?"

He was so weak, he was unable to reply.

Moments before the police arrived, he told her in a whisper that he had been the victim of an attack.

Who had attacked him, and when, and what exactly had happened, asked Lillian. Was he hurt?

"No, I'm not hurt." At last he sat up.

Ten minutes after Walt had called, three officers from Beverly Hills precinct 208 arrived at the house. The victim made a report. And even though the officers remained quite polite, and treated him with respect and reverence, still it seemed to him they didn't really believe what he was telling them. Over their radios, they called in to ask for any information there might be regarding a Bill or William or Wilhelm Dantine. But I wasn't listed in Los Angeles, or anywhere else in California, I had spent the last seven years living in various places out of state, and had only recently returned to Hollywood. The policemen made a search of the garden, but found no further evidence of anything, beyond a couple of spatters of yellow paint on a rhododendron bush.

They promised Walt that they would send in a team of experts early in the week to perform some forensic tests. He asked them to undertake a thorough search of the entire garden, but that request was politely ignored.

Lillian attributed her husband's collapse to his continual overwork. The recent land purchases in Florida and the stress to do with the setting up of the New World in Orlando, had indeed taken a lot out of him.

Walt took to his bed. He remained in his room for the rest of the day. Lillian called her daughters, Diane and Sharon. They both did as their mother asked, and came by Carolwood Drive. Their father, however, declined to see them. "Not today . . ." he wheezed through the bedroom door, his voice was very weak. "Please, not today . . ."

In the late afternoon, the still hissing locomotive started to move forward along the narrow tracks. All at once, in slow motion, and all by itself.

CHAPTER FIVE

My visit to Walt's garden doesn't appear in any newspaper article, magazine essay, or in any of the numerous biographies that have appeared over the years about my one-time employer. The family closed ranks and remained absolutely silent on the subject. More, they asked the authorities who were handling the case not to let any information whatsoever leak out.

The team of investigators who took up their work a few days after the incident, found traces of blood, identified paint spatters, and was able to pick up hairs of Jonathan's and mine, as well as a box of crayons that fell out of my pocket as we were making our getaway. Since I had been arrested and fingerprinted in New York some years back over some driving offense, I was established beyond a shadow of a doubt as the owner of the box of crayons.

In the meantime, my last place of residence had been investigated as well. For the past four years we had lived in Chicago, where I made a modest living as a painter and carpenter. The apartment we lived in was just off Tripp Avenue, no more than a couple of hundred yards from the house where Walt was born, in a part of town that by the mid-sixties was rapidly degenerating into a slum. We had moved back to Los Angeles only two months before. My father readily gave the policeman who came knocking on his door information as to where I might be found: I was in the Silver Lake district of town. Martha and I were renting a little bungalow in the hope of being able to afford a larger, nicer house before long.

I was arrested in the early evening of October 11, before the eyes of my wife and sons, just as we were sitting down to dinner. The two policemen had been issued a search warrant, and came up with a small quantity of marijuana in the bedroom. Martha and I were in the habit of smoking the occasional joint in the evening.

With sirens and flashing lights, I was driven down to the main police administrative building in downtown L.A., on Pershing Square. There, for the next three hours, I was subjected to an extremely disagreeable interrogation, almost entirely devoted to my professional career and personal life since leaving Walt's studio, and with remarkably little attention to my actions of October 9, 1966.

To my surprise, though, I was allowed to go home that same evening, at around 11 p.m., after Martha had deposited a bond of two thousand five hundred dollars. (My father loaned us the money, he always had cash hidden at home, and when Martha turned up on his doorstep in the evening and told him what had happened, he reluctantly pulled out a stash of hundred-dollar bills from under the mattress, and handed them to his daughter-in-law with the words: "There'll be trouble if I haven't got this back in a month!") A year later, I was charged with illegal possession of drugs. It cost me a criminal record and a hefty fine—it took me four years to pay it all off.

I realized only weeks after my arrest why I hadn't been put behind bars and why bail hadn't been set at a higher figure: Walt had not wanted to press charges, even though the team of investigators had all it needed to convict me. I often asked Hazel why he had been so astonishingly lenient with me. To begin with, she said she didn't know.

"Why didn't you insist?" I kept up the pressure. "'Walt,' you should have said to him, 'How can you let this fellow go after what he did?'"

"He didn't want the thing blown up. He was afraid of the press," she finally admitted. "Afraid someone might get a whiff of the story. That's the only reason he let you alone. There were times when he was real sorry that you were still at large."

The police at least felt the need to frighten me and my family, to teach me a lesson. Hence my sudden arrest and interrogation. At that time, in the mid-sixties, at the beginning of the Hippie and Underground movements, anyone who swam against the stream was regarded as a potential subversive. Thank God I was too old for the draft. The authorities in California would have liked nothing better than to pack me off to Vietnam.

My brush with the law didn't faze me much. I was more amused than anything. But weeks later, Martha was still in a state of shock. She couldn't get over it. She tormented herself and me with bitter reproaches and threatened repeatedly to leave me. She failed to show up for work for several days, and it almost cost her her job as a typist in an ambitious new aeronautical plant. If she had lost it, that would have been a calamity for us all. There was no way that I would go with my hand out to my rich father, who had successfully sold his dry-cleaning business to an immigrant family from Taiwan. Basically, it was my wife's income that kept us going. At that time I wasn't able to make much of a financial contribution. Since my feelings about Walt Disney didn't diminish in intensity after his death—if anything, I was even more at their mercy then—we had no choice but to separate, and later, to get a divorce.

My sons suffered badly from the shake-up of our family. Ted, the younger, broke off relations with me after Martha and I split up. He went to live in Canada in 1980, and is running a hotel complex near Vancouver, which has something of a name in winter sports circles. It's been years since I last saw him. We manage to talk on the phone for a couple of minutes every New Year's Day. The conversations are always identical.

In the years following my arrest, I began to familiarize myself with my victim's biography in the same way that exegetes study the Bible, or entomologists endeavor to grasp the cellular makeup of, say, an ant. I made approaches to the circle of his acquaintances (he had no close friends, or only very few), collected articles and interviews, read accounts by contemporaries who had met him. Out of the floods of available data, I should like to quote two items. The Soviet film-magician Sergei Eisenstein, who had visited Walt in 1940 in Hollywood, wrote in an essay on Disney's work: "It's as simple as that: the mighty, international, global, ageless popularity of the little hero Mickey Mouse, drawn by the great artist and master Walt Disney, has overtaken America's other great Walt—which is to say, Whitman." Walt had evidently deceived Eisenstein into believing he was the creator of his animations, the inventor of his protagonists. Then, in Thomas Mann's diaries, I found the following entry for April 9, 1938: "Lunchtime, taken in Walt Disney's car to his studios. Tour, followed by screening of the film *The Magician's Apprentice* in a crudely drawn state. Remarkable personality, D's. Onset of fatigue. I remain near silent." My assumption that Disney didn't even know the name of Thomas Mann, much less any of his books, turns out to have been quite wrong. Not only did he know my idol, he had talked to him, asked him for his views, shaken hands with him, spent hours in his presence!

*

Not long after my arrest, I read a small item in the press, stating that Walt was to be awarded the highest honor of the National Forestry Association at the end of October in Williamsburg, Virginia. At the very last moment, I decided against following him out to the East Coast, partly on account of Martha, who found out about my plan (I had unwisely mentioned it to Jonathan). My other reason for declining to visit the state of Jefferson and Madison was probably my fear of being identified and rearrested in Williamsburg. I had no reason to suppose Walt would show himself to be merciful a second time.

Still, thanks to the efforts of a couple of eyewitnesses, I was substantially able to reconstruct the three days he spent in Virginia. Phil Jester, the former president of the National Forestry Association, with whom I got in contact a few years ago, told me as much as he could remember. And Hazel George was once again of inestimable value to me. She accompanied Walt to Williamsburg, because he was desperate not to have to suffer any more of the shooting pains without her being there to minister to him. When Lillian heard that her husband's nurse was to accompany them on their trip, she promptly started to unpack her half-packed suitcase on the bed. Her profound aversion to Hazel came from the time when, on rare occasions, Walt still used to succumb to temptations.

Miss George was ten or perhaps fifteen years older than I was. She never let me know her date of birth. She bore a certain resemblance to a sergeant major—both externally, with her pockmarked skin and her short haircut, and in her manner too, which was rarely gentle or caressing. Even so—and why should I deny it, particularly at this stage—I lived with her for a time after my separation from Martha. But only for a short time. A real relationship with me, she told me, was impossible. My rage and disappointment over the loss of my career in animation, plus what she termed my paranoid obsession with Walt, made me, she said, all but unbearable.

For her part, she could be like a wild beast when we fought, or as soon as she got on to the subject of someone she feared or despised, or who had disappointed her. On the other hand, she remained strangely motionless and very silent when we slept together. We probably performed the sexual act (I am reluctant to call it making love) no more than six or seven times. Hazel referred to it as "the nasty thing," not just in the context of our own endeavors, but generally. Talking of her first lover, an electrician who had fallen in World War II, she used to say, "Frederick always wanted to do the nasty thing with me. I was almost relieved when he got shipped out to Europe."

I asked her on various occasions how often "the nasty thing" had happened between her and Walt. In the first years of our acquaintance, she avoided giving me a reply. But by and by I persuaded her to give in and satisfy my curiosity. "The nasty thing happened very rarely with Walt. He wasn't really interested in it. Also he wasn't very strong, you know, down there. Lillian would have been aware of that early on. Why do you think Sharon was adopted? Because he practically stopped sleeping with his wife once Diane was born. It was a pretty awful thing to do, so far as he was concerned. Even being with Lillian before they had Diane, he often told me, was something he never really enjoyed. All those things that people do together, he found basically disgusting. On that point, we were very much alike, Walt and I."

It must have been the same for Disney's father, too: "Daddy only slept with Mummy once a year, if that," Walt told Hazel, "and that was usually in March, when the first warm days swept across the country." To back up his theory, he drew attention to the fact that, of the five Disney children, four—namely Ruth, Herbert, Raymond, and himself—were born in December. Lillian and Walt evidently observed the tradition—their Diane was also a December baby. When his wife insisted on getting a girl for adoption, he made it a condition that she, too, have been born in December. Sharon's birthday, on December 31, 1936, commended her to her adoptive father.

"Sharon played a great part in his life," Hazel informed me. "To him, she was the most pleasing of all women. And from the time she was twelve or thirteen, he could barely restrain himself from giving her visible proof of his adoration. And other than that? Well, there's the rumor that, in or around 1948, he had a fling with the Mexican actress, Dolores Del Rio. I must say, it makes me laugh. That lady was deeply unappealing to him. He told me that many times. No: Walt and love, those two words don't go together. At least, not sexual love. To be left in peace by the ladies—that was his greatest desire."

I voiced my suspicion that he might have felt more comfortable in male company than around women.

"More comfortable? Sure, I'm sure he was more comfortable," Hazel replied. "But if you're trying to suggest he had ever *done* anything with a

man, then you're dead wrong. That's even more far-fetched than the idea
of him having a fling with Del Rio! There was a rumor going round the
studio once that he and J. Edgar Hoover were an item! What nonsense!
Hogwash, as Walt would say. Sure, he helped the F.B.I. track down Communists, and of course he was on close personal terms with Hoover. But
sex? With *men?* Sooner shoot himself in the leg, any day!"

*

In the weeks following my visitation, Walt was in a state of nervous ten-
sion and fatigue as bad as any he'd ever known, apart from the breakdown he suffered in 1931. Then, it had taken just one wrong word from a
colleague or his wife, or irritation over the least bit of sloppiness to cause
him to burst into tears, real howling fits that could go on for ten or even
twenty minutes. It was like that this time, too. Lillian was heard to say to
her daughter Sharon: "I just can't take him any more."

On October 28, 1966, the day before he was scheduled to leave for
Williamsburg, Walt went over to St. Joseph's Hospital on Buena Vista
Avenue, just across the street, for a general medical checkup, finally fulfilling the promise he had made Hazel six weeks before. Blood and urine
samples were taken, and detailed x-rays of the neck, shoulder, and pel-
vic area made. His heart was auscultated and found to be sound. Circulation, respiratory system, and reflexes were all thoroughly examined by
the medical staff. The complete test results, the doctors agreed, would
be presented to him on his return from Virginia.

The next morning, Walt, Hazel, Sharon, and Victoria, Sharon's nine-
month-old baby girl, set off on the journey to the East Coast. When the
little company jet, a Grumman Gulfstream, built in 1964, had reached
its cruising altitude, Disney suddenly screamed: "These pains are going
to kill me one day!" Sharon got up and went over to him, kissed him on
the brow.

"It's my leg! My shoulder! My neck!"

Hazel poured him a glass of whiskey. And, thirty-three thousand feet over Nevada and Arizona, gave him a massage.

Victoria cried almost uninterruptedly for the whole six-hour flight. Walt smoked one cigarette after the other. Once, Sharon leaned down to him: "Daddy, please stop doing that. It would make you feel so much better."

"Come on, honey, you've got to allow a man to have at least one vice!" He took hold of her hand and stroked it.

The party was met by Phil Jester, the good-humored president of the National Forestry Association, at the little airport in Williamsburg. As had been arranged, he took them back to the foundation's guest house on the edge of town.

Belle Aire, a pretty two-story Colonial mansion from the latter part of the seventeenth century, situated on the bank of the James River, had once been a well-known cotton plantation. I visited there a few years back, so as to be able to see with my own eyes the place where Walt went just three weeks after my attack.

It was raining on the evening of October 29. It was dark already by the time they arrived. The only view from the windows was of the broad river by moonlight, and the tall old oaks, planes, and sycamores that stood around the inn. They went to bed early. Walt's room was on the ground floor. Sharon and the baby were upstairs. Hazel's room was next to Sharon's.

Walt woke up at half past four the next morning, in spite of having taken a couple of strong sleeping pills the night before, and having drunk more than half a bottle of Cutty Sark. Breaking with his usual habits, he switched on the TV. CBS was carrying reports from South Vietnam. The day before, President Johnson had visited the military base at Cam Ranh and the American soldiers stationed there. Surrounded by enthusiastic GIs, he grinned and waved, gave out autographs, and promised them: "As soon as the Communist aggression from the North ends, we're out of here!" Cheers from the thousand soldiers. General Westmoreland clasped both of Johnson's hands, thanked him for the surprise visit, which took just two hours and twenty-four minutes, all told. There followed an interview with the president's wife, Lady Bird Johnson, recorded in a hotel suite in Manila. Mrs. Johnson is sitting on the extreme edge of a deep and soft armchair. The room is filled with the shouts of a crowd of demonstrators who have gathered in front of the hotel: "Go-home-*John*-son! Go-home-*John*-son!" The chanting gets louder and louder. Mrs. Johnson smiles weakly: "They remind me of the fans when Texas plays Oklahoma." Asked what moment on her journey to the Far East had left the most lasting impression on her, the president's wife replies: "What I liked best was the sheep farm in New Zealand that we saw last week. We were able to watch a whole flock of sheep being shorn. You must remember: I'm a country girl at heart . . ." Followed by commercials: the new 1967 Chrysler, the Newport 440 TNT model. Pall Mall, new luxury length, outstanding . . . and they are mild! Pepsi-Cola cold! Pepsi pours it on! Anahist cough syrup. When a cold attacks you, fight back with Anahist.

He switched the television off.

His hot bath that morning brought him no relief. The pains in his hips, legs, and neck were so strong that Walt reached for the most powerful drug he carried in his personal traveling pharmacy: Codeine. Its one side effect was that it generally made him dizzy, but he didn't mind that. He was used to a faint reeling sensation in his head. For over twenty years he had been mixing prescription drugs and alcohol, taking sleeping pills and sedatives, washing them down with bourbon or scotch. This soft swaying, this drifting along walls, and the constant feeling of fatigue in his limbs—all that he had become accustomed to, and it was in no way disagreeable to him, a dreamy sort of slow-motion surfing.

He shambled slowly up the stairs to the first floor, at six in the morning, on Sunday, October 30. Victoria was sitting in the middle of the room when her grandfather walked in. She laughed at him. Sharon appeared to be fast asleep.

"Coochie coochie coochie coo!" whispered Walt, and stroked the little girl's straight blond hair. "You sweet thing. Is your mama still asleep? Your sweet, pretty mama. Do you know how much I love your mama? More than the whole world. She's the prettiest, sweetest, kindest, nicest woman I've ever known. See her lying there asleep, isn't she sweet? The smell of her hair. Come on, shall we wake her up?"

"I'm already awake." Sharon's quiet voice was heard from under the covers. "Tell me, Dad, . . . what do you have against Diane?"

The river burbled, and he heard the calls of the birds that hadn't yet migrated to warmer weather. It was still raining. With every gust of wind, the trees lost hundreds of dark red, yellow, beige, brown leaves.

"Daddy?"

"Yes, my darling?"

"What have you got against Diane?"

"Why are you asking me that?"

"Your not loving her hurts her very much."

"I do love her."

"That's not true."

"Can I give you a kiss?"

"Only if you answer my question first."

He looked out the window. He loved watching the leaves fall, it reminded him of Marceline.

"Daddy? Aren't you going to answer?"

"Diane is a lot like my father."

"And you hold that against her?"

"I don't hold anything against her, Sharon."

"Your father. I only have the vaguest memories of him. I was four when he died. But Elias wasn't as awful as you always pretend he was. It's really not true. Aunt Ruth says he used to play the fiddle incredibly well. Hillbilly songs and cheerful tunes. No one who plays the fiddle like that, Ruth says, can be an altogether bad man . . ."

"Can we skip that?"

"Absolutely not, Daddy. I want to know more, I don't want you to keep interrupting me halfway. As soon as something concerns *you*, the person you truly are, you change the subject."

"I have to prepare a talk for tonight. Will you help me?"

"Only if you give me an answer."

"I already gave you an answer."

"You're avoiding the point, Dad."

"I can't really say any more. Diane . . . she's my daughter. But you, you're more than that. To me." With a great effort he crouched down next to the bed and kissed Sharon on the temple. Let her long blond hair slip through his fingers. "I love you more than any other being on this earth . . ."

"That's a sin against Diane and Mom."

"Lillian worships the ground I walk on!"

"I wouldn't be so sure . . ."

Victoria gurgled, played with a Davy Crockett doll that carried a silver-plated rifle over its shoulder. Before he got up off the floor, Walt pressed his head against Sharon's once more.

It was two years before that his daughter had married a Kansas City–born architect-to-be by the name of Bob Brown. During the ceremony, her adoptive father had wept for several minutes. Lillian had nudged him, and urged him to show some self-control. The assembled guests in the Beverly Hills town hall all pretended not to notice anything. Everyone knew he had a way of crying over next to nothing, for instance when viewing the first run-through of a new scene his people showed him on a Moviola, or when listening to the country-and-western music of his favorite singer Fred Rose, or simply when he was sitting in the cinema, in the theater, in a concert hall. But his tears had never flowed so uncontrollably as at Sharon's wedding—everyone who was there was in agreement about that.

*

At nine in the morning, Phil Jester drove up, as planned, to take the group on a sightseeing tour. Hazel refused to go. When Walt asked her what the matter was, she turned away and ran into her room.

In the three hours in which Jester took Walt, Sharon, and the baby around, he barely stopped to draw breath. He proudly showed the visitors through the splendid buildings dating back to the Colonial era, and only restored in the mid-thirties, thanks to a grant from John D. Rockefeller. Walt admired the beautiful, well-tended gardens and parks of the car-free town, and the almost Disneyland-like production of a past that seemingly rose up to meet you everywhere. The town fathers of Williamsburg employed several dozen young men and women to appear all day in period costume, playing the farmers, artisans, soldiers, and lawyers of the pioneer era.

To tourists who recognized him, Walt gave out autographs. In the court building of the former capital of Virginia, he allowed himself to be photographed in the stocks. I have the picture—he looks utterly miserable, his eyes closed, his mouth contorted in pain, like someone who's been tortured for days and nights. He was putting on the expression to convey the way a man clapped in irons by the state, and condemned to death, must feel. In fact, the photograph completely accords with his actual emotional state at the time.

When they got back to the Belle Aire Inn in the early afternoon, Hazel George was no different from when they had left her. Walt asked her to give him some hot compresses, and she stalked angrily after him into his room. He asked what the matter was. She didn't say anything.

He went on asking until, finally, she gave in: "The walls here are paper-thin, you know that?"

He understood right away. Didn't let on, though: "What do you mean by that?"

"I suggest that in the future you have Mrs. Brown see to all those things … that are especially close to your heart."

"She's my daughter."

"She's no more related to you than I am."

"Her maiden name is Disney. I've worshiped her since she was twelve years old . . ."

Hazel burst into tears. In all the years I knew her, I never once knew her to cry in my presence.

"I love Sharon endlessly. And that's the truth."

"And just the other day, in the laughing room," Hazel said very loudly, "I seem to remember you saying that *I* was the most important person in the world for you. After Roy."

"I'd be lost without you."

"You're only saying that because you want your massage."

In the hope of winning Hazel's sympathy, he turned the subject to me: "I should have insisted on having that demon put behind bars." He sighed, buried his face in his hands, even tried a little heave of the shoulders. "I'm so scared. What if he comes again . . . !"

"He won't come again," she comforted him.

"How can you be so sure?" Walt's voice sounded at once gentle and fragile. "The blood! Ooh, that horrible blood!"

"Walt, calm down! Come on, now, stretch out . . ."

And that was how easy it was for him to get Hazel to forget her anger.

*

That evening, at a banquet for over a hundred guests, Walt received the medal of the National Forestry Association: "In honor of your extraordinary life's work, and its role in preserving the natural resources of North America," as the official commendation read.

"We are particularly honored this evening," Phil Jester began, "to be able to have in our midst a man who has achieved something rather extraordinary: something that no one in any of the world's biological or zoological laboratories would have believed possible. He has given animals a soul. And only since Walt Disney's films has mankind understood that nature is only lent to us while we are here, and that we have the responsibility to care for it as we might care for a brother, a living being, a friend . . ."

After the main course (pheasant, polenta croquettes, zucchini, served with a Cabernet Sauvignon from one of Virginia's prestige wineries) and before the chocolate cake dessert was served, Walt rose to address those present, who were seated at twelve large, round tables. He had had neither the time nor the peace of mind in which to prepare a speech. He gripped the back of his chair and saw one hundred and ten pairs of eyes aimed in his direction. Such situations always reminded him of the night before the opening of Disneyland, on July 13, 1955, which was also his thirtieth wedding anniversary. The moment that he walked out on the stage, to address the gala audience. He had drunk a good many glasses of gin and tonic in the preceding hours. He felt so proud and so happy! Then he had looked around, seen the silhouettes of the people surrounding him, waiting for his words, and had remained silent. Beamed all over his face, radiating energy and happiness. He allowed the audience to share in his joy without uttering one single sentence. In the end, Lillian, Sharon, and Diane had clambered up to the stage, and escorted him to the car, driven him home. He sat in the back, clutching a map of Disneyland in one hand, and a mouse balloon in the other. He was still grinning like a loon. He looked like an eight-year-old.

That evening in Williamsburg, October 30, 1966, he would also have preferred not to say a word. But then, after a long silence, he launched into an improvised speech that went on for six minutes, on the subject of his passion for nature. He talked about Marceline, about his discovery there of woods and fields and meadows and ponds. About his fascination with animals, wild and tame alike. About hunting for mushrooms, roots, and herbs, about how he reached with his bare arm into the Wolf River to catch trout. He closed with the words he invariably used at such appearances, no matter how many times his family, his closest associates, and his advisers would beg him not always to stick to the same formula wherever he went: "I have remained a farmer's boy all my life. A country boy, hiding behind a mouse and a duck . . ."

The guests at the banquet applauded, banged their fists on the table in approval, and finally rose to show Walt what they thought of him by giving him a standing ovation. He sat down, he had tears in his eyes. The tears overflowed the rims of his eyes, they trickled down his cheeks, down the side of his neck, and disappeared into the collar of his frilly dress shirt.

The journey back to California was supposed to begin the next morning. Unexpectedly, at the end of the gala evening, Walt turned to his host to ask if it might be possible to spend an extra twenty-four hours in Williamsburg, he liked it so much. Phil Jester was delighted to think that his guest of honor would be spending another day in the former plantation house at Belle Aire.

Sharon was less happy with her father's decision. She wanted to get home, had promised her husband that she would be back by the evening of October 31 at the latest. But she gave in. Flying back to California other than in Walt's private jet seemed far too complicated an undertaking to her.

Hazel, meanwhile, was quite content to stay longer. On Monday, the 31st, even though it was continuing to rain heavily, she went for a long walk along the banks of the James River. Got as far as the confluence with the York, the other big river that flows into the Atlantic near Williamsburg. The paths were covered with autumn leaves, she drew in their moldy aroma, strode across an endless, thick, colorful carpet of leaves. It was late afternoon when she returned and found Walt, Sharon, and Victoria all asleep.

About half an hour after Hazel's return, the doorbell rang.

"What a nice surprise!" Hazel tried hard to give Phil Jester the feeling that he was welcome.

He was awkward, a little embarrassed: "I'm sorry . . . turning up unannounced . . ."

"But we're your guests here!"

Now divorced from his wife, he lived on his own in a spacious villa that had been handed down in his family over several generations. He wanted, he explained as he took off his wet raincoat, not to spend the evening on his own. Hazel led him to the inn's living room. He had brought with him some "goodies" as he described the contents of his large sack, leftovers from yesterday's banquet, packed into several "doggy bags."

He asked what the Disney family was up to.

Hazel knocked on Walt's door. He didn't answer. She went in, shook him until he woke up. It felt like the middle of the night to him. His head was spinning. When she told him the actual time, and that Jester was waiting in the living room, he groaned, wailed, got up, groggy as a bear waking from hibernation. He asked to have Sharon brought in to see him. Hazel refused point-blank to wake her, much less take her in to him. Slowly he got dressed, his long sleep weighed on his neck and chest like lead. A lead armoring that he couldn't possibly take off. He dragged himself upstairs. Sharon was up, but didn't want to leave her room. She gave her father permission to take the baby down. He was incapable of carrying Victoria, and she couldn't walk on her own. Crossly, Sharon brushed out her long blond hair. Finally, she came down to the living room with Victoria and Walt.

Jester put out plates, glasses, silverware, cloth napkins, lit some candles, and served the cold dinner. They sat down, Walt at one end of the table, Jester at the other. Phil tried to make conversation, talked about what a "magnificent success" the evening had been. No one replied. He seemed to be talking for his own benefit, into space, into a void. He changed the subject, enthused about *Bambi*, *Dumbo*, *Peter Pan*, and *Mary Poppins*, stressed how happy these films had made his son Steven, who for three years now had been living in Seattle with his mother, Jester's ex-wife. They listened, but didn't respond. Hazel managed a few pleasantries, not very convincingly. There were groans, sighs, whispers. Victoria burrowed into her mother's lap. Walt had his right elbow on the table, his forearm straight up, and his chin resting in his cupped hand. In that position, his neck was a little less painful.

The doorbell rang. No visitors were expected. Hazel got up to see who it was, but the door didn't have a peephole. "Who is it?" she asked through the locked door. "It's me," said a child's voice.

"Who are you?"

"I'm Lucy."

"What do you want?" Hazel was still speaking through the door.

Walt had got up to see who it was, and stood behind Hazel. "Won't you open the door?"

"I wanted to see who it was first."

"Trick or treat!" called the child's voice.

"Of course! It's Halloween!" Hazel turned to face Walt. It had completely slipped their minds.

"Trick or treat!" the child called out again.

Finally, Hazel opened the door. The rain was streaming down, yet the air had a late summer warmth to it. In front of them stood a screech owl, small, dark, and wet, with long blond curls. The curls were what first struck Walt, and only then the owl mask and the beige-, brown-, gray-, and white-feathered owl cloak. Hazel took a few steps outside to see if any adult was accompanying the child. But Lucy had come on her own. She stood in the hall, perfectly still. The rain dripped off her, and formed a little puddle at her feet.

"Er, one moment . . . I'll just go get something, you wait here." Walt vanished into his room.

"Wouldn't you like to . . . dry off a bit?" asked Hazel, and led the girl into the living room.

Sharon screamed. There was nothing playful about this, she was so shocked when the girl walked in. On her mother's lap, Victoria started wailing, louder and louder, as she had done on the flight.

"Couldn't you *please* take off that hideous mask?" Sharon asked the visitor.

"What's your name again?" asked Phil.

"Lucy." She pushed back the uncannily realistic night owl mask, so it perched somewhere between her brow and the top of her head, and the pointed yellow beak stuck up into the air like the horn of a unicorn. Her dense clustered curls were pressed flat by the gray-white mask. Lucy was pretty, and strangely precocious-looking. Her blue eyes shone from deep within.

"Where do you live?" asked Phil.

"On Colonel Clark Street," replied Lucy.

"Where's that?"

"Not far from here. Do you know where Wilcox is?"

"I've lived in Williamsburg for twenty years but I've never heard of those two streets."

"Anyway, that's where I live!" the girl replied.

"And how old are you?" asked Sharon.

"Eight and a half."

Sharon had managed to quiet Victoria. "What about your parents?" she asked. "Do they just let you wander around the streets on your own? Aren't they scared at all?"

"Scared? *My* parents?"

"Yes. Your parents."

Lucy didn't give any answer.

By now, Walt had gone through his room, or rather turned it upside down, in the hope of finding some little something. There was nothing there. Upstairs as well, in Sharon's room and Hazel's, he went through drawers, cupboards, looked in suitcases and bags. In the whole planter's villa, there wasn't so much as a pack of chewing gum. Phil Jester had brought fruit with him for dessert. To think that, of all the citizens of the United States of America, Walt Disney didn't have a single treat to give a child on Halloween! How was it possible to forget something like that? They should have gone out and bought something during the day. But neither Sharon nor Hazel had thought to buy any treats. If Jester hadn't shown up, there wouldn't have been anything in the house to eat for them either. Maybe more children would come along in the course of the evening. Word must have got out that the King of Kids was staying in Belle Aire. What a catastrophe for his image! There was a chance that this little bit of forgetfulness would get into the papers and cost him dearly. He could see the headline: "Unsweet Uncle!"

He called down the staircase for help. He had another look around, this time with Hazel. And again found nothing. Then suddenly he had the idea of giving Lucy the ballpoint pen he kept in his shirt pocket. It was half plexiglass, the clear half containing a pale-blue fluid. Mickey was sitting in a little rowboat, and the boat was drifting toward a huge Niagara-like waterfall. If you held the pen at an angle, it looked as though Mickey was managing to row just hard enough to defeat the current. Walt sighed with relief.

"But we'll have trouble if any more kids show up," he remarked to Hazel, as they went down the stairs.

"You'll think of something, you always do."

They returned to the living room, where there was a deathly silence.

Walt gave the girl her present. "Here, Lucy, I've got something for you. It's not a sweet, but I hope you'll think it *is* sweet."

She looked at the ballpoint.

"Well, aren't you going to say thank you?" asked Sharon.

"Do you know who the nice man is who gave you that?" put in Phil.

The girl shook her tousled blond head.

"He's the father of Mickey Mouse."

Lucy showed no reaction.

"Have you ever heard of Walt Disney?" asked Walt Disney.

She stared fixedly at the laid table, the cold leftovers, the glinting wine glasses.

". . . or Donald Duck . . . ?" added Walt.

"No."

Sharon pushed her chair back, walked right up to the little girl. "Will you do me a favor?"

Lucy popped her present down a slit in her owl costume. Looked expressionlessly up at Mrs. Brown.

Sharon was unexpectedly loud: "Go away. Go away right now. I want you gone. Now. Right away. Get out of here! Go!"

Lucy put on her mask. The head of the raptor, the king of the night, as the owl is sometimes called, was really uncommonly accurately reproduced. The ears looked so genuine, the way they stuck up into the air in little points, you could think you had a genuine horned owl in front of you.

"I want this girl out of here!" Sharon started yelling: "Daddy, make her go! I don't want her here any more!"

Lucy ran to the door. And slammed it shut behind her.

Sharon walked back to the table, hugged her daughter, and sobbed.

"For God's sake!" Walt was beside himself. "Just because she didn't know who I was? So what! Why should every single child in the world have to know!"

"I *so* wanted us not to stay here another night!" Sharon gave Hazel a contemptuous look. She picked up her baby, and disappeared upstairs.

Walt, Hazel, and Phil were left on their own. And drank whiskey, all three of them.

All at once, Disney softly began: "When I was eighteen, Hazel knows this story, I came across a fortune-teller at this big birthday party in Kansas City. She took me aside and predicted: 'You will die at the age of thirty-five!' I absolutely believed her. And I was astonished to reach my thirty-sixth birthday. And it wasn't for another ten years after that that her gypsy curse finally faded from my mind. I was flying in this tiny plane with Sharon, who was thirteen at the time, and with this drunk pilot, over Alaska. We got caught in a storm. It got so bad, we almost came down. We had to crash-land. The little propeller plane broke in two. And from

that time on, I've felt immortal. Why am I telling you this story? Well
... Lucy made me happy. Very happy. She sort of ... released me. She
helped me overcome a demon ... to defeat this force.... Hazel, I think
you're right: he won't be back! You need to drive out Satan with
Beelzebub. Lucy was a gift of fate ... my only chance ..."

"May I ask ... ?" ventured Phil Jester.

Walt interrupted him: "I don't want to say any more on the subject."

Half an hour later, the guest got up, mumbled a quiet thank you.

"We should be thanking you! If you hadn't turned up, Phil, we wouldn't
have known where to get anything to eat. It's a good thing you came!"
Walt called after him, as he climbed into his Buick station wagon: "And
please excuse my daughter's behavior. She does sometimes behave like
a child."

Belle Aire was all on its own on the edge of town. There were no other
houses anywhere around. That evening, no one else made their way to
the National Forestry Association guest house, on the banks of the James
River. The doorbell didn't ring another time.

*

"The following morning I started making inquiries, because of course I
was mystified. The little girl named streets that didn't exist, not in
Williamburg," recalled Phil Jester when I looked him up, several years
later, in a run-down old folks home on Main Street in Richmond, Virginia. He had got in trouble with the law for selling illegal gaming li-
censes, and lost all his property. "No one had heard of the girl in either
of the two elementary schools in town. Several times I walked the streets
near the guest house. Then, just a few hundred yards from Belle Aire
plantation, I saw this mobile home. I'd noticed it before, but this time I
heard the loud wailing of a woman's voice. I walked closer, feeling just
like my boyhood hero Tom Sawyer when he gets into one of his scrapes.
I called out: 'Lucy?' just to see what would happen. The narrow door

swung open. 'What are you doing here? Who are you?' It turned out that the very young couple who lived there did indeed have a daughter called Lucy. She had been missing for several days now. I helped the parents, who were both illiterate, to initiate a police search. I was taken in and questioned, because I was one of those who had met the girl. If I'm not mistaken, Mr. Disney was sent a letter about her as well. When I went back two or three days later, to see if she might have turned up, there was nothing where the mobile home had been but an empty patch of grass. I asked the sheriff what had happened. He didn't know either. He was astonished. Neither the authorities in Williamsburg nor I have seen or heard the slightest trace of Lucy or her parents since."

CHAPTER SIX

On Wednesday, November 2, 1966, Walt Disney was presented with the results of the medical tests he had undergone a week before.

"I come from a religious background, Mr. Disney." Slowly, a little fussily, Dr. Aron Silverstein laid out several files in front of Walt. "My father was a Talmud scholar in Cracow. Do you know where that is? No? Well, Cracow is in Poland," he went on, a gaunt, rather humorless man with thick glasses and whitish-gray hair cropped short. It was hard to tell his age—fifty, perhaps, fifty-five. "In our tradition, we don't agree to an operation until we've had three separate opinions. I'm assuming that a little lump in the left lung that shows up in the x-ray may not be benign. I should like to remove it as quickly as possible. Your blood count also gives me some cause for concern. The convenient location of St. Joseph's to your studio shouldn't stand in the way of your soliciting further professional opinions, should you desire to do so."

Since returning from Williamsburg, Walt had felt oddly fresh and light. The three days in Virginia had been almost like a holiday for him. Silverstein's assessment of his overall condition therefore came as a surprise and a shock to him. He asked to see the x-ray. In speaking of a little lump, the doctor had wanted to protect him from the truth. The growth was at least two and a half inches in diameter.

"I don't know much about your religion, Dr. Silverstein. I appreciate your advising me to get other opinions. But I'm a man of gut instinct. Always have been. I've gone a long way on instinct, no one can deny that. I'm grateful to my destiny. I know that this shadow I see here needs to go, and as soon as possible. I don't need to hear any further interpretation."

"Are you a heavy smoker?"

Walt was just reaching for a pack of Gitanes when the doctor put his question. He left his hand in his jacket pocket.

"I would suggest you come in next Monday." Dr. Silverstein buzzed for his senior nurse, and asked her to enter the name of Disney, Walt, born December 5, 1901, place of birth Chicago, profession film producer, in his calendar. "Ah, I see . . . you've got your sixty-fifth coming up! Well, you'll be as good as new by then."

"We're working on a huge theme park, in Florida," he explained to the doctor, "a hundred and fifty times bigger than Disneyland. Every day counts, every hour is precious. My brother Roy can't do all the work by himself."

"In two or three weeks, we'll have you back on your side of the street, you'll see."

"That's impossible! I can't afford such a long interruption."

"Mary? Will you put Mr. Disney in suite 401, so he can enjoy the best view of his studio."

Walt didn't tell Lillian, or his daughters, or Roy, how serious his situation was. He thought it prudent to make his approaching hospitalization appear as trivial as possible, and ideally to keep it completely secret. The Disney firm had gone public in 1940, and ever since, except for a few trivial setbacks, had made bigger and bigger profits. He was afraid that if news of his condition got out, it could do serious, if not irreparable, damage to the share price.

The official version was that he had to go into the hospital for a few days, to get his disk realigned, possibly also to undergo an operation on his neck muscles, because the pain in his back and shoulders had become unbearable. It was only to Hazel that he told the truth, on the evening of November 3, in the laughing chamber.

"That doctor you recommended to me, across the street . . ."

"Was he satisfied with you?"

"They found this . . . sort of lump . . . on my lung. He wants to whip the damned thing out ASAP."

"Oh my God!"

"I thought you would help me be calm about it!"

"It could be benign, I suppose."

"Hazel, please. I can feel this damned shadow all around me. I can sense there's been something wrong with me ever since that devil set foot in my garden."

"I don't see the connection."

"My guess is every reasonably successful man has an archenemy, someone who makes it his business to persecute him. Usually he won't even know. Someone who reveres you and despises you at the same time. Who dogs your every step with his envy. Who won't let go. Not until you're six feet under."

"Walt, only two days ago in Williamsburg, you were saying the exact opposite, you were saying that little Lucy—well, I didn't quite understand what you were getting at—but you said something about her having set you free. Released. Something . . . ?"

"Yes, that's right, I did think that."

"It'll all turn out fine, I'm sure."

"You're right. It'll turn out . . . fine."

*

He moved into suite 401 on the afternoon of Sunday, November 6, at around six o'clock, accompanied by his wife and daughters, who left him at nine. Slept extremely badly, dreamed about me, saw me standing in front of him, naked, bleeding, with flashing razor blades in my hand. I rushed up to him and slashed his wrists. He looked down at his lacerated arms, and saw nothing but the two deep cuts. He was surprised not to see any blood. He woke up not knowing where he was, fell asleep again, and had the same dream all over again.

The harsh neon light beside the bed yanked his eyelids up at six o'clock on Monday morning. Was it his execution? Sister Mary handed him his white gown. A funeral gown? She gave him a sedative injection, and announced that he would be taken into the operating room in one hour. Half-asleep, he waited. Saw himself all alone in deep snow, on the edge of Marceline. His hands, his feet kept getting colder. His pulse was rapid. The drug, if anything, heightened the dread that raced through his veins. Burning, flame, dart of fire, amid the icy cold.

A young man in a green gown, with a bad squint entered the room, bowed low to Walt, whispered: "I love Dopey best!" He lifted the body gibbering now with cold onto a metal bed on large, inflated rubber tires. Laid a thin blanket over it. Trundled him down long corridors to an enormous elevator. Lillian bent down over Walt, it was a very long time since she had got up so early. She planted a kiss on his cold forehead, didn't say anything. Waved to him as he was wheeled into the elevator. She still supposed he was just going in for a minor neck or back operation. Silverstein had fulfilled Walt's wishes, and kept the truth even from his closest family.

The short ride up to the sixth floor of the clinic. The operating room. His body juddering violently from his head through his chest down to his toes. His feet and legs bare. Silverstein and his team of four assistants, all in green surgical masks, surround him; the anesthetist injects the drug into the vein in the crook of his elbow. Walt sees covered mouths, chalk-white noses, and flashing knives, scissors, needles. He looks up at the big tall windows, just like the ones in his studio, he sees the permanently blue, cloudless sky of Hollywood. A private jet crosses his field of vision. The four brilliant round lights over the operating table—the last thing he takes in before his eyelids drop. But he isn't asleep. Hears every word. He feels, smells his chest being rubbed with disinfectant fluids. He is far colder now than that other time, with Hazel, in the laughing chamber, playing the squirrel game. He can clearly sense the places being marked with a pen where the surgeon is going to cut him open. He must give the doctors some sign, even if it's just raising his little finger: he must let them know that he's still awake. A limitless terror spreads through his brain: they could begin cutting open his body before the anesthetic has had a chance to work. He is unable to lift his little finger, move his toes, his lips, or open his eyelids. They will begin the operation, he thinks over and over, before I'm asleep! He tries to roll his eyes, as he always has, in order to wake from the nightmare that torments him. And remains rigid. Deathly still. He can hear and feel and smell everything. Lying impassive on his back. A pen sketches another arc over his right nipple. He has never known such fear, not even in Alaska, when the little single-propeller airplane almost crashed. "What have I done to deserve such punishment? In my films the sky looks bluer than it is in reality, the grass greener, the people kinder. Is that wrong? Have I perpetrated some sin? What's my crime?" he cries out to himself, in his fear. "I have made people happy. My works have made them laugh, put millions of people in a good mood. Who could claim they're not my works?"

And then at last the anesthetic kicks in.

*

He came to three hours later, in the intensive care unit. They had had to take out the whole of the left lung, Silverstein told him, when he opened his eyes briefly. They fell shut again. He slept, for many hours, and was woken by the whimpering of a boy in the bed next to his. The thirteen-year-old had had an emergency operation—he'd broken his pelvis playing football at school. Walt asked the nurses on duty to tell the boy who his neighbor was, if there was a good moment. And then he fell asleep again.

Meanwhile, Lillian and the daughters had a meeting with Dr. Silverstein in his ultraplush office. He no longer stuck to the confidentiality agreement; in fact, he plunged the whole family into a state of frantic despair.

"My worst fears have been realized," the doctor lectured them in dramatic tones. "We may expect any number of metastases in the very near future."

Lillian gasped for air, for words: "But . . . his back . . . I thought . . ."

"Your husband wanted to spare you the worst."

"He's got . . . *cancer*?"

"In an advanced stage."

"Oh my God! How long has he . . . ?"

"Mr. Disney might live . . . another two years."

"Only *two* years?"

"Two years . . . at the most."

"But how can he do everything he's planning to do in just two years?"

"Perhaps," Silverstein suggested, "he's made too many plans."

*

When Walt woke up late in the afternoon, his neighbor in intensive care spoke to him. The boy was feeling quite a bit better than he had at noontime: "I can't believe I'm lying next to you, sir. The sisters told me. I can't believe it. Wait until I tell my friends at school. None of them will believe it. None of them will believe how lucky I am!"

"You call that lucky? Lying in a hospital with a broken pelvis?"

"Of course it's lucky, sir, because I'm lying here beside you. I've just been watching you sleep. I'm very interested in all your movements, you see, because I want to be a doctor when I grow up, maybe a vet, maybe a pediatrician, and I'm interested in the tiniest movements, both with animals and people."

"Can I make a suggestion: be a vet."

"Why's that, sir?"

"You know my films. Why do you think I mostly have animals as the heroes of my stories?"

The boy didn't know. He waited patiently for Walt to tell him.

"Some of the most fascinating people I've ever met are animals . . ."

The boy chuckled. "Animals give me a funny feeling, sir. But it's a feeling I like!"

"My wife won't let me keep a pet at home. She's terribly strict, you know? We had a big brown poodle. We called her D.D., for Duchess Disney. But ever since she died . . . I'd so like to have a dog again."

"You've *got* to have a dog again."

"You're absolutely right. But try telling my wife that."

"I've got a Dalmatian puppy!"

"I envy you. If you can keep a secret, I'll tell you something."

"Word of honor, Mr. Disney, on the life of my dog!"

"OK, but you're not to laugh at me."

"Of course I won't!"

"Ever since I was a boy, I had this feeling in my right wrist . . . I don't know how to explain it to you . . . an almost painful feeling, a stabbing, cramping feeling each time I see an especially cute little animal or baby animal."

"Why would I laugh about that? I think that's very interesting!"

"With every puppy, every little deer or lamb, even piglets when they suddenly realize how funny they are as they're horsing around. . . . No sooner do I see that, the creature as it truly is, so to speak, than I feel that stabbing, that cramping in my wrist! Every time! Isn't that strange? And I've yet to meet someone who had the same thing."

"And does that never happen to you with humans, with babies?"

"Good question. No, not once." He stopped for a while. And went on: "What's he called, your Dalmatian?"

"Pongo, of course, because of Pongo and Perdita in the *101 Dalmatians*."

"Really? I like it! And what about you? What's your name?"

"Josh. Josh Lowry."

"Mr. Disney!" chided Miss Bowers, the nurse on duty, a pretty girl from Wyoming. She had been listening behind the door for the past ten minutes, "And Josh! You two, quiet now! You're not to talk so much. Tomorrow maybe. That's enough for today!"

*

"Good morning!" said the boy, when Walt opened his eyes the following day, just after sunrise.

"Good morning, Josh."

"I couldn't sleep, I stayed awake most of the night thinking: How do you manage to draw so much, sir?!"

"We don't need the 'sir.' Just call me Walt . . ."

"You see, in one of my comic books it said that two million drawings were made just for *Snow White* alone, even if they weren't all in the finished film. Is that really true? And then all those hundreds and hundreds of your other films, long and short. And then my favorites, *Bambi* and the *101 Dalmatians*. All those millions and millions of drawings! I expect you must have a couple of people to help you with them. Am I right? And then the film about animals in the wilderness, *The Desert Lives*, or the one about the seal island in Alaska, I've seen quite a lot of your documentaries! And all the Mickey Mouse comics! Every week there's a new issue with new stories, week after week, about Donald, who's my all-time favorite of course, and Donald's nephews, and Uncle Scrooge, and . . . and the Beagle Boys, and the amazing Gyro Gearloose. How do you manage to do it all?"

"He made me feel really awkward," Walt told Hazel later. "I admitted that, well, I no longer drew *everything* myself. But I couldn't possibly tell him I'd never drawn so much as a single figure, not to mention a whole moving sequence myself."

"But then you do at least think up all the jokes and ideas yourself?" Josh went on.

"No, Josh, not all of them. For example, if I'd had to draw all of *Snow White* by myself, it would have taken me two hundred and thirty years, working round the clock, with no breaks. Five hundred men and women were involved on *Snow White*, which is still my favorite of all my films."

The boy looked at Walt. Was silent for a long time. "But then what exactly *do* you do?" he finally asked.

"Well, I guess I'm kind of like a bee: I go from one part of the studio to another, collecting pollen. I give encouragement and motivation to my men. You could say I fertilize them."

"I see." Josh seemed disappointed. "You fertilize them . . . like a bee . . . buzzbuzzbuzz . . ."

"That's right . . ."

Silverstein walked into the intensive care unit at the head of a team of assistant doctors, announced in a loud voice that he was very pleased with the success of the operation. Walt would be able to return to his suite as early as tomorrow. "You're a great patient, Mr. Disney, I congratulate you on your recovery. But you've got to promise me one thing."

"Cigarettes?"

"A promise?"

"I promise you . . . and myself too." And then he said in a whisper: "Can I ask you a favor?"

"Don't be shy. It's not in your nature!"

"I'd like to talk to you, alone. As soon as possible."

"I'm afraid today's not possible, but we can talk about whatever it is tomorrow," Silverstein nodded benevolently. "Sure thing."

The next day, Walt was wheeled back into suite 401. He received a telegram from John Wayne, who had had to undergo a similar operation himself a few months before: "Welcome to the one-lung club! Here's to a long, healthy life for you and me. Yours, John." How could Wayne know the true reason for Walt's hospitalization if his own family didn't know it? When Lillian and Roy came to visit him that morning, he learned of Dr. Silverstein's indiscretion. The rage he flew into can't have done much for his recovery.

When the doctor came by on his rounds, this time without his many assistants, he bent down to his patient and inquired: "Well, how's it going? How do we feel? Here I am, on my own, just the way you wanted."

Disney replied: "You completely disregarded my request to keep this secret!"

"Is *that* what you wanted to tell me privately?"

"I had something I wanted to ask you. But it's taken care of, thank you very much."

"Mr. Disney, please. Don't be sore with me. Surely you don't think it's possible to keep an operation of this magnitude a secret from your own family?"

"I would have told my wife the truth. But I would have liked to choose the time myself."

"What was it you wanted to ask me for? I promise I'll keep your secret."

Walt turned away, and asked Silverstein to leave him alone. He wanted to rest.

*

Four days after the operation, he was able to get up, and walked the corridors. Nicotine deprivation was what got to him the worst. They gave him drugs to try and suppress the addiction, but the drugs didn't help much. On one of his little outings, on the third floor, he ran into Josh, who was taking his first few steps with the help of a walking frame.

"Like a bee . . . buzzbuzzbuzz . . ." said the boy.

"But without my ideas, without my participation, nothing, absolutely nothing would have resulted. Do you understand that?"

"I understand. You're like God. People put your ideas into effect."

"That's er . . . that's kind of the way it is. I can see someone's potential. And then I get him to put it down on paper!"

"Are you a happy god?"

"Sometimes, Josh."

"When were you happiest?"

"I can tell you that without the shadow of a doubt."

"Tell me!"

"It was at the big railway exhibit in Chicago, in the city where I was born. With authentic old locomotives on a great wide music hall stage. There was a painted backdrop of a beautiful landscape, with the shore of a little lake. All the locomotives were steaming, and you were even allowed to drive them! I was there with my friend Ward Kimball. Can you imagine what a fantastic time we had? They had whole trains on show from the olden days. And Ward and I were allowed to steer some, even a Tom Thumb, for instance, a Central 999, a DeWitt Clinton. There was even a John Bull. Never in my life was I as happy as in those three days in the spring of 1948, at the Chicago Railroad Fair. And I know for a fact that that's where I first had the idea for an amusement park of a superior kind, an inspiration that led directly to my kingdom in Anaheim."

"And I was just going to tell you that the best moment in my life was last year."

"Go on."

"I spent the entire day with my parents at Disneyland, on my twelfth birthday. That was the happiest moment of *my* life."

"As soon as you get out of here," promised Walt, "you must come and visit the land of your dreams again. That's an invitation, all right?"

"All right, Mr. Buzzbuzzbuzz!"

The next day, Walt made his way down to the third floor again, hoping to see his young friend. But he couldn't find him. He asked a nurse if she knew where Josh Lowry was. Had he already been sent home?

"His parents picked him up this morning, " she said. "So far as I know, he's being transferred to Westwood, to the Hospital at UCLA."

Walt was displeased. As though Josh's parents had needed to get his permission before taking such a step. Brusquely, he asked for information: "Were there complications then?"

"I'm sorry, sir. I'm afraid I can't tell you."

"Come on, you can tell *me!*"

"Not even you, sir."

"Is it because you don't know, or because you're not allowed to say?"

"Both, sir."

*

On the sixth day after the operation, Walt told Hazel, who was visiting him twice a day, "I really do feel like a new man! Silver-Guy was right." The cigarette addiction seemed overcome, and much faster than he would have thought possible.

"Such nonsense, those doctors' disgusting pessimism: only two years to live! It's outrageous, don't you think?"

Hazel George nodded emphatically. And added: "Even so, I put Silverstein in the picture."

"In the picture?"

"About your wish."

"What wish are you talking about?"

"The thing you most fervently desire."

"Silver-Guy?"

"He's your doctor."

"But I don't trust the man. You know that."

It was their first fight in years. Hazel reminded Walt that she had promised to do what she could to assure him of his cryobiological future. How could she carry out his dearly held wish, and in the teeth of opposition from his family, if she didn't consult with the surgeon who was treating him?

"I wanted to talk it over with Roy again to take some of the weight off your shoulders, my precious," he groaned, as the vehemence of their argument gradually subsided.

"But you should have told me."

"What was Silverstein's response?"

"Very positive indeed."

"You're just saying that to humor me."

"No, he's read the same literature you have. He told me your wishes exactly suited his intentions. He's buried your diseased lung in ice, so that at some future date . . . he says you can never know. You're in the very best hands, with him. For several years now, he's been looking into the possibility of deep-freezing people who have passed away. And he promised me he would be discreet this time. Not one word will be allowed to leak out. That's in his own interests too, he said. And anyway, you're going to live for many, many years yet."

Walt forgave her. It was his fault for placing too heavy a burden of responsibility on her. Clearly, she had to talk to someone. "I promised him," Hazel concluded, "that you'd give him confirmation that it's me he'll have to deal with in this regard one day, not Lillian."

"I will give him that in writing. I certainly will." He got up, went over to the big window, where the air-conditioner was blowing its icy blasts, and looked out at his studio, across the street.

"Curious," he muttered to himself, "to be indebted to a Jew for my everlasting life. Extraordinary people. Always managing to take the limelight. Make themselves indispensable . . ."

In the course of the next few days, there was a frank discussion between Walt Disney and Aron Silverstein. The doctor assured his patient that their agreement would remain totally confidential—neither the family nor the media would be told anything. The information would be withheld for one full year after his death, when it would be released with much fanfare.

"Now please don't give it another thought," Hazel heard the doctor call out to Walt as he left the suite. "You will be cured. In a few days, you'll be able to go back to your normal life!"

The pain from the slowly healing surgical incision was intense. Each time he laughed, he felt like he'd been stabbed.

*

I managed to keep informed regarding Walt's condition in the days and weeks immediately after my visitation. Ward Kimball, with whom I'd remained on friendly terms ever since my dismissal (I never let him know of my fascination with his boss's biography, though), told me casually that Walt had been admitted to the hospital shortly after his return from Williamsburg. Kimball knew nothing of what had occurred in the garden of the villa in Holmby Hills, as I ascertained by a series of carefully couched leading questions. All he knew was that the boss had some health problems—in fact, he called me in mid-November to let me know that Walt had been operated on just the week before.

I drove to Burbank, and first spent a long time walking back and forth outside the hospital, opposite my former workplace. I hadn't been there for years, it was just too painful to see the studio in all its glory, the surrounding streets and houses, the wonderful chain of mountains on the nearby horizon. At the pushcart, which was still where it always was, I bought myself some of Walt's favorite snack, a palm-sized red and white box of peanuts. After an hour of aimlessly walking around, I made up my mind to go into St. Joseph's. I wandered from floor to floor. It felt like I was invisible. The danger of being identified struck me as minimal, not least because after my arrest I'd shaved off my beard and had my hair cut short. No one asked me what I was doing. Even though the nation had been deeply scarred by the Kennedy assassination in the fall of 1963, the rich, famous, and powerful were still astonishingly unprotected and exposed in the mid-sixties. It wasn't until 1968, with the murders of Robert Kennedy and Martin Luther King, that things started to change. Another five years on, and the stunt I pulled off on my thirtieth birthday would have been impossible.

I thought I would turn up in Walt's suite, stare at him in silence for a few seconds, and then leave. But just as I got to the half-open door of suite 401, my heart was beating so hard that I contented myself with just flitting past the door. Even so, I was able to see that Walt appeared to be asleep. Roy, who was wearing a suit similar to the one he'd had on in Marceline, seemed suddenly aged, his head like a skull covered with parchment. He was standing by the foot of the bed, and was gripping his brother's right ankle; in his other hand he was balancing a little stack of papers and giving them his whole attention. I don't know if they were telegrams, letters, sales figures, or bank statements. Brief as it was, that one moment will always be with me.

I left the hospital and drove off in the direction of the San Gabriel Mountains. After about twenty minutes I reached a plateau, the Tujunga Canyon pass. I parked the car on a steep slope and tramped through difficult terrain, brush and dried cacti and thornbushes. A smell of peppermint and chamomile. I went on and on, for miles, until I got caught in a thicket and lost my way. My arms and cheeks, my back and my forehead were all badly scratched.

The more pain I felt, the deeper I penetrated into the needle-sharp, razor-edged holly brush. Then it was evening, and I had great trouble finding my car again in the dark.

CHAPTER SEVEN

Barely two weeks after the operation, Walt let it be known that he wanted to leave St. Joseph's. He couldn't stand it any longer. To nurses, doctors, and family members he complained of boredom for the first time in his life. Silverstein warned the patient that there was a possibility of a relapse in the weeks ahead. In any case, the convalescent would have to drastically reduce his normal workload.

On Monday, November 21, he crossed Buena Vista Avenue and set foot in his studio for the first time in over two weeks. From the looks he got from his entire staff he saw how radically his appearance must have altered. Everyone who saw him was shocked. His cheeks sunken, his usually roundish face shapeless, collapsed. No one said anything— and everyone sensed it: Walt Disney, a marked man.

If anyone asked him about the time in the hospital, he would invariably reply: "Very well. The doctors there are terrific. They whipped out a lung. Now I'm a new man. I've got it all under control!" He showed everyone John Wayne's telegram. He was very proud of it. He carried it with him everywhere, in the inside pocket of his jacket.

In one of the long corridors, he ran into Chuck Amen. In the few weeks since they'd been in Anaheim together, the Disneyland technician had lost fifteen, sixteen pounds. He looked great. Walt didn't mention the change in the young man. They discussed the continuing closure of the Abraham Lincoln exhibit. As Walt limped off slowly, he turned around: "Farewell, Chuck." Amen was startled. His boss was never usually one for such formality; at the most, he would say, "See ya later!"

The first letter Walt dictated to his personal assistant, Tommie Wilck, was to Josh. He asked him if he and his parents would like to spend the weekend before Christmas, December 17 and 18, in the Magic Kingdom, staying in the Presidential Suite at the Disneyland Hotel, welcomed by Walt in person, and, whenever possible, accompanied by him. The reply from the boy's mother reached the office two days later: Josh had died on Wednesday, November 17, from a rare form of bone cancer. Every time Walt asked the question (and he asked it often): "Any word from the Lowrys?" Miss Wilcks replied: "Nothing yet!"

"Are you sure you sent that letter to the right address?"

"Positive, Walt."

"Then try them again. You don't get an invitation like that every day of the week!"

*

"One less lung, so what?" kidded Peter Ustinov, during a break in the filming of the comedy *Blackbeard's Ghost*, in which he was playing the part of the ghost of a pirate, who comes back to haunt the inhabitants of a small fishing village. Walt visited the set just two days after checking himself out of the hospital. "The only problem," the actor continued, ripping the false beard off his cheeks, "is if you want to go mountaineering. It's not the strain, mind you! It's the thin air, *that's* what you can't take with only one lung!" Ustinov was appalled at Walt's emaciated appearance, but didn't let it show. "It was as if his cheeks had melted away," he said, describing his impression to me years later. "It was like ... like butter melting. And his charming smile, which I always loved about him, had turned into a kind of grimace."

They discussed one of their pet projects, something that had been in the works for years, and was now only waiting for a mutually satisfactory script: a film to be called *Nikita Khrushchev's Visit.* What would have happened, goes the plotline, if the Soviet premier *had* managed after all to pull off his planned visit in the fall of 1959, circumventing the U.S. State Department's ban. Disguised as a street sweeper, he wangles his way past American secret service agents and anti-Soviet demonstrators, and, in the middle of the night, creeps incognito into the kingdom of dreams.

"When are we finally going to make our film, Walt?" Ustinov asked. "I really want to play fat Nikita. All the more as he's the spitting image of my mother."

"I never knew your mother was bald!" Walt always had to laugh when he was with Ustinov.

"Now, in all seriousness, Mr. Disney, how far along is the script?" Ustinov wouldn't let go, partly because he really did want to play Khrushchev, partly to give Walt the impression that he still had an absolute, unbroken faith in the powers of the Burbank magician.

"I know you'll understand, Peter. But until the time when I'm fully myself again, and have overcome all the handicaps of my illness, I want to conserve my energy for the project that, for the time being, is more important to me than anything else."

During the days in the hospital, he had resolved that he would, for now, devote all his attention to EPCOT, the futuristic model town that he planned to integrate into his new Floridian kingdom one day; blueprints for tomorrow's world would be evolved in a creative collaboration between architects, town planners, and industrialists. In the course of the last few months, feelers had already gone out to General Electric, Bell Telephone, General Motors, IBM, and Westinghouse. Disney had envisioned a town in which all traffic would be routed underground, where parks and pedestrian precincts dominated, where the paramount consideration was the quality of life. New modes of public transport would be tried out, daring and original architectural ideas realized.

Walt's decision toward the end of 1966 to make EPCOT his priority project was driven not least by the reflection that his cryobiological plans might benefit from being placed in a wider context, sheltered in a fully integrated scheme in a way that would make it harder for his family to oppose them when it came to it. He would be the first man to have his mortal remains frozen in the name of medical progress, in a predesignated place in the heart of the experimental community of EPCOT, where there would no longer be deaths and burials in the established form.

To conduct his research into futuristic living arrangements, he withdrew into a little room on the top floor of the studio, which he had had converted by some of his personnel into a new study exclusively dedicated to the EPCOT project. Over the past years, this space had been used as a storeroom for old editing tables, empty film cans, old recorders, antiquated spotlights—things that would probably never be used again. No one in the building could bring themselves to throw these things away. One of the cameras there, an Arriflex from the forties, had last seen action in the filming of *Mary Poppins*. It was a talisman, something of both sentimental and museum value, and quite possibly possessed magic powers.

During his stay in suite 401, the two windows of this attic room had been in his field of vision. Now, though, he found himself looking out from the one-time junkroom across at the hospital, a man on the mend, someone whose fortunes had changed, and who was well on the way to new shores.

Among other literature, Walt read the books of the architect Victor Gruen with, for him, an unusual intensity. He read *The Heart of Our Cities*, for instance, and *Out of a Fair, a City*, works that had to do with the crisis that had begun to affect American inner cities from the mid-sixties on. On the one hand, ever heavier automobile traffic was choking the life out of them, and on the other, they were increasingly deserted after office hours, because they offered so little in the way of places to meet, so few amenities of the sort that were to be found in the center of most European cities. Gruen's solution was to Europeanize the cities of North America. He was an advocate of pedestrian zones with pavement cafes, small food shops, parks, public benches, and playgrounds for the children. He dreamed of a renaissance of the city, of the city center in particular, a rebirth of the "heart," as he liked to describe the focal point of a city. Gruen became the father of the mall, the roofed-in shopping center. He was the creator of the first such center in 1956, in Minnesota, a completely regulated environment, immune to all forms of precipitation and temperature variation, of the kind that was to be copied hundreds and thousands of times all over the country, filling their inventor with shame and rage. The more of these town-sized shopping centers there were, the more deserted the actual city centers became; with his own invention, Gruen had actually accelerated the decay of the inner city that he had wanted to reverse. One consequence, though, of his initiative to pedestrianize the city is that from the late sixties, a growing number of cities in Europe and the United States started introducing car-free zones.

"I want to see Marty, right away!" Walt yelled down the telecom, instructing his secretary to send up one of his most important imagineers. *Imagineers* was his word for those technicians, builders, and designers, who realized his ideas in the form of audio-animatronic figures, Disneyland attractions, and other mobile sensations, and Marty Sklar was one of the best of the breed.

"Does the name Victor Gruen mean anything to you?" he asked the young man, of whom he was particuarly fond.

"No, Walt. Never heard of him."

Disney showed him some of Gruen's books, let him flip through them for a moment, and then went on: "I want you to find out where the guy lives. And whether he'd like to talk to us. I'm really impressed by what I've been reading. He has a real vision."

"Here, Walt, on the jacket it says: 'Was born and grew up in Vienna, Austria. Came to the U.S. in 1938.'"

"Yes? So?"

"Well, doesn't it bother you that . . . ?"

"That what?"

"Never mind." He broke off. "Where would you like to meet him?"

"I can't really travel at the moment. If possible, he should come here, to us."

"Not to your home . . ."

"Marty, the separation between working life and private life is sacrosanct. Let me know as soon as you have any news!"

*

The following evening, on Thursday, November 24, at the house of Diane and her husband, the former professional football player Ron Miller, and their six children, Thanksgiving was celebrated. Sharon, Bob Brown, and little Victoria were also present, as were Roy and Edna, with their son, Roy Edward. Walt and Lillian felt proud to be patriarch and matriarch of this extended family of sixteen.

Before they all sat down to eat, Walt whispered to Diane that she had better find a different place for his nephew, because he had no intention of sitting next to him. In his view, the thirty-six-year-old was dull, stupid, lacking in passion and imagination, ". . . and for all that, incredibly pleased with himself!" as he often remarked. Walt was afraid that sooner or later, when the Disney brothers were no longer around, the young man would want to take over the company.

While the turkey and stuffing were consumed, served with pumpkin pie and plum pudding, potato, sweet-potato and onion-mash, celery hearts, and cranberries, Walt said barely a word. He had brought one of Victor Gruen's writings with him to the table, an essay in the professional journal *Architectural Vision* on the subject of public transportation in the future, and kept throwing covert glances at the text, to Lillian's evident annoyance. The reading glasses he had recently had to start wearing, and which he then refused to take off, even for longer interruptions in his reading, bothered her no end—even more than the fact that he took no part in the conversation.

"They make you look like an East Coast intellectual," she jeered. "That's not my Walt." Both daughters laughed and agreed with her. Only Roy, who also wore glasses, and had done so for years, and not just for reading, stuck up for his brother.

Walt excused himself after the main course, lay down on a sofa nearby. His grandchildren left their places, thronged around him, were called back by their parents, kept jumping up again, and so on, until the result was a commotion of coming and going and laughing and shouting, which did a little to lighten the atmosphere.

Lillian, though, remained in a state of rare gloom. "That Thanksgiving evening," she was to write in a letter to Ward Kimball, "for the first time, it was impossible to stop yourself from thinking that Walt might only be with us another couple of years. We had all felt very optimistic when he left the hospital, but only a few days later we were afraid the doctor might be right with his gloomy outlook."

At eleven o'clock that night, the phone rang. Walt was sleepy, not least on account of the many medicines he had had to take earlier.

"Marty Sklar for you," Diane said to her groggy father.

"Boss, I'm sorry to call you so late, but I thought you'd like to know that Gruen is living in Los Angeles at the moment."

"Who is?"

"Victor Gruen."

"Can he ..." Walt sat up, with a little difficulty. "Can he come and see us?"

"As soon as possible!"

"Tomorrow?"

"I'm not sure your family would like that, if he came ..."

"You're right."

"Better wait until after Thanksgiving weekend."

"Monday, Marty. First thing."

"Good night, boss. And all the best."

"All the best, Mar—"

Sklar had already hung up, such was his embarrassment at disturbing Ron and Diane Disney Miller during the holiday.

*

The meeting between Walt Disney and Victor Gruen took place in the former storage room, now EPCOT workroom. At half past eight, Gruen arrived in Walt's office on the first floor, where he was met by Marty Sklar, who took him on a ten-minute tour of the building, and showed him around some of the various departments. Then the two men climbed the wide staircase up to the fourth floor and knocked on the door of the corner room.

Gruen was wearing a dark blue suit and a pale-blue shirt. He only ever wore bow ties. Over the years he had bought himself three hundred and sixty-six of them, so as to be able to leave home in different neckwear every day of the year, leap years included. A head shorter than Walt, and heavily built, almost fat, he looked the picture of health in comparison to Disney's frail, emaciated form. And yet, the architect, born in 1903, was only two years younger than the man he had come to see.

"Of course, the moment I walked into that attic room, I thought: this man is very ill," Gruen was to tell me in the Viennese Café Bräunerhof, at the end of the nineteen-sixties. "On the other hand, he had so much enthusiasm, and was so incredibly taken with my ideas, that I rapidly forgot my initial impression, and permitted myself to be swept up and carried along by his charisma. One thing I can tell you, Wilhelm—you don't mind, do you? After all, I did know your parents before the war—whatever you may think of him today, there are very few people I've truly admired. I can count them on the fingers of one hand. Walt Disney is definitely one of them. He had incredible charm, even when he was so ill. And, without ever saying a lot, he could get you to give your best, the very best you didn't know you had. I'm sure I'm not the first to say so, but he wasn't just charismatic. It was much more than that—he had an uncanny gift of making people creative."

As for his part, Walt told Hazel that at the moment of their first meeting he was unable to repress a certain antipathy toward his visitor. Marty Sklar also noticed right away that his boss didn't feel quite at ease with the architect and town planner. Anyone who knew Disney well could tell from a twitch about the mouth, as with a cat or a hunting dog sniffing some unfamiliar scent. Gruen, in his appearance, reminded Disney of his long-time rival Max Fleischer. Also born in Vienna, he emigrated to America round about the turn of the century, and grew up in the States. For decades he observed Disney with hatred and malice, saw in him the man who had got in the way of his own fame, and referred to him as "an intellectually undistinguished saccharine manufacturer from the Midwest," putting his own creations, say, Popeye the sailor, or Betty Boop, on a much higher pedestal than Mickey, Donald, and Goofy. Another factor was the way Walt was able to woo away a number of Fleischer's best draftsmen over the years, among them my closest colleagues on *Sleeping Beauty*—Mark Timmerman and Sidney Frost. In the mid-fifties, Walt happened to offer Max Fleischer's son, the director Richard Fleischer, the feature *Twenty Thousand Leagues Under the Sea*, with James Mason, Kirk Douglas, and Peter Lorre as the leads. The young man's response was cool: out of loyalty to his father, he was unable to accept the offer. "Ask him, maybe he won't mind," was Walt's suggestion. And Richard Fleischer did just that. "You *have* to do it, you'd be crazy to turn down an offer like that!" was Max Fleischer's response, "and tell Mr. Disney he shows good taste in his choice of directors." At the end of the shoot, Walt asked his

long-time enemy to pay him a visit in Anaheim, took him around Disneyland for a day as his guest of honor, and the outcome was that the two
gentlemen not only made peace, but became friends of a sort.

As soon as Disney and Gruen had sat down across from one another,
with Marty as the quiet observer in a corner of the little room, Walt's
inhibitions fell away. A window was thrown open in St. Joseph's, and
reflected its dazzling light into the little EPCOT garret.

"Well, it was hardly a conversation in the accepted sense," was Victor
Gruen's verdict on his meeting with Walt. We spoke German together,
Gruen and myself, I can still hear his voice clearly in my head. It was
like the sound of my mother's voice when she recited to me the parts she'd
once played on the stages of Vienna. "It was more of a monologue on the
part of Mr. Disney, in which he gave me his description of an ideal future
city. The surprising thing about it was that he touched on all those aspects of the subject that had always mattered most to me in my work:
such things as car-free, bustling inner cities, streets for pedestrians, with
special attention paid to bridges, because bridges are my great passion,
little rivers, parks, all the things I dreamed of and partly wrote about in
my books. And then, at last, after fifteen minutes, a question: 'How would
you like to build the ideal city for me?' I was on fire, you can imagine.
The dream of any architect. The perfect situation par excellence. Of course,
he asked me to talk about this or that detail. He was curious to hear what
my concept of a graveyard for the future might be—an aspect I must con-
fess I hadn't ever thought of before. I advocated—not realizing at the time
how much this must have chimed with his own views!—not burying the
dead, but putting them in refrigerators, in the hope of one day being able
to overcome every disease and death itself. I didn't leave with a signed contract in my pocket. But I was completely convinced I would be the chief
planner and commissioning architect of EPCOT. I think I have rarely been
as happy as I was on that November day in 1966."

From Hazel I learned that the two men had also spent a long time
talking about the period before the war, when the young architecture

student still went by the name of Victor Grünbaum, and had been in-volved with a small group of friends in a political cabaret that performed once a month in a cellar on Naschmarkt, where it poked fun at the new masters in Berlin and warned of the dangers of National Socialism. Aus-tria, still independent at the time, though it was under the heel of the right-wing authoritarian Chancellor Kurt von Schuschnigg, would fall victim to Hitler unless people woke up—that was the basic message being put across in Grünbaum's shows.

When I asked Victor Gruen about that part of his encounter with Walt, he seemed surprised: "How do you know what we talked about, he and I? And if you do know, why bother asking me?"

I repeated my plea, with all the charm and urgency I could muster, to tell me everything he could remember.

"Are you writing a book about Disney? Or making a film about him? Why go into so much detail? If you must know, the story I told him took place in the days of the Anschluss in March 1938. Once Hitler marched into Vienna, people like us in the cabaret were of course at the top of every list of undesirables. You will have heard that often enough from your parents. I called my wife every other hour, or even every hour, to make sure that things were all right at home. And during one of these calls, Litzi whispered into the phone: 'The Gestapo are just searching our apartment!' I ran through the city, right along the Bräunerstrasse, right here, where we're sitting now, and across the Michaelerplatz and through the Hofburg. I ran down to the Naschmarkt as fast as my legs could carry me. Finally, completely out of breath, I slipped into our cellar cabaret through a back door—I always carried a key with me. In our tiny dressing-room, there was a trunk under the mirror containing all our costumes. One of these was an SS officer's uniform, black, creepy, but smart. I took a few seconds to slip into it, gazed in horror at my reflection, and ran out on to the street. No one suspected anything. On the contrary, a mili-tary vehicle screeched to a halt when I gave a signal to it. German sol-diers followed my orders to drive me to the station! I had told my wife to try and get to the station with the most important books, my slide rule, and the money we kept in the safe at home. She was there. Of course she was aghast when she saw me in my uniform! But we managed to get to Landeck in the Tirol. And then, after adventures, like those of the Trapp family in *The Sound of Music*, we got across the Alps into Switzerland. On foot, of course."

"How did Disney react to your story?" I asked.

"You really want to hear about every time someone *breathed*, don't you? Well, first, he was very quiet. Oddly quiet, almost. It was as though the whole thing were, somehow . . . unpleasant to him. Then he said: too bad he hadn't produced *The Sound of Music*. It had been a huge success the year before, and they used his lead from *Mary Poppins*, Julie Andrews. The only other thing he said, on the subject of Vienna, was that he had been there just once, during the filming of the Lipizzaner film, *Flight of the White Stallions*, which was set during the Nazi period. Oh, and one other thing: that right next to a place where he grew up and had a happy childhood, in Missouri, there was a village just about a mile away, called Wien, not even Vienna, but Wien, Missouri, where he had often gone as a boy, because it had the biggest church for miles around. And because, even though he had a practically areligious upbringing, he still liked to sit on his own in the silent church."

"He didn't say anything," I interrupted him, "about having had an employee who came from Vienna?"

"You mean, did he talk about you? No, not a word."

I could feel myself flinching, and the blood shot up into my face.

"And after that, we returned to matters that had to do with EPCOT," Gruen continued. "'I want to see you again in about a month,' he said, 'just before New Year's. And you're to show me your first sketches. Then you can go and talk to my brother about a contract. Don't be too modest in your demands. My brother offers everyone peanuts. Don't pay any attention to his whining. You should ask for ten times what he offers you. And I want you to give this job more energy and undivided attention than you have ever brought to any project. It's worth it!' and with those words he let me go. I was walking on air."

"Wien, Missouri, eh?" I asked.

"Wien, Missouri," replied Victor Gruen.

*

On the evening of November 28, Walt asked his wife to accompany him to Palm Springs. He had the feeling that a few days on the Disney ranch, in the mild, dry desert air, with a stack of books, would do him good.

The private airplane took off from Burbank airport, and soon veered away to the southeast. The flight took only twenty minutes. Walt went forward to the cockpit.

"Kel," he said to Kelvin Bailey, his long-serving pilot, "you know I've just spent some time over in St. Joseph's. I'm not a well man. So they tell me, anyway. Shouldn't have thrown myself back into my work so quick, I suppose. But once I'm in Palm Springs, I always feel better. I'll stay there until I've fully recovered. Then we'll phone, and you can come and get me. When will that be? I haven't a clue."

Bailey wasn't expecting to hear from his employer for another two or three weeks at least. But two days later, on November 30, Walt felt terrible. His pain was so bad that he decided he would have to put himself through another examination.

"Kel? It's me." His voice sounded frail. At first the young man didn't recognize his boss on the phone.

At Palm Springs airport, Lillian and Walt asked the chauffeur to drive right up to the plane. Mrs. Disney helped her husband out of the car, he couldn't have managed by himself. And on the gangway up to the plane, he clutched the handrail and made his way up slowly, very slowly.

Back in Burbank, in the late evening, he was met by the studio limousine, and taken straight from the airport to the hospital.

CHAPTER EIGHT

Suite 401 had been kept reserved. Dr. Silverstein assumed that his most famous patient might well be returning to St. Joseph's before the year was out. Admittedly, to see him again so soon was something of a surprise even to him. The doctor thought it wasn't a good idea to operate again immediately. Nor was he in favor of radiation treatment, with radioactive isotopes. Walt needed to get his strength up, he told the family, before he could be exposed to such treatment. He gave him a shot of morphine to ease the pain.

Walt dreamed for days and nights. He drank little, ate little or nothing, and grew weaker and weaker. Lillian and the daughters moved into a room on the fourth floor, and, whenever they could, took turns spending the night at the hospital.

On Monday, December 5, 1966, his sixty-fifth birthday, he woke at nine o'clock, to find Lillian, Diane, and Sharon standing round his hospital bed, singing his favorite song: "This old man, he played one, he played knickknack with his son, with a knickknack-paddiwhack, give a dog a bone, this old man came rolling home," all ten verses of it, to "he played knickknack with his hen."

He looked right through them. "But I'm not an old man," he whispered. "Why did you call me an old man?" And fell asleep again.

In the afternoon, Hazel came. Roy had just left. Walt hadn't been awake during his brother's visit. When he saw his confidante, for the first time that day a smile flickered across his face.

"I always thought when life was over, you stopped remembering the past," he murmured. "But I can see every step and hear every word, feel every pain and smell every scent that was my life."

"You are alive, Walt, please!"

"I can distinguish good and evil with the same clarity, and I don't want to ignore either the good or the evil."

"What evil are you talking about? There's no evil in you. Anyway, it's your birthday, my friend, you're sixty-five today!"

"I'm still attached to my past life, just like a newborn baby is attached to its mother, until the umbilical cord is cut."

"You haven't died, Walt. Listen to me!"

"Or am I still alive? Will I live forever?"

"You will live forever."

She handed him a kaleidoscope. He held it to his eye, and turned and turned it, and let continents and oceans, planets and solar systems and galaxies, let the universe whirl past his gaze.

"Probably didn't even cost you five dollars, right?" Only now did he come out of his trance.

"One dollar, seventy-five, if you really want to know."

"And it's worth more to me than my first car that I bought in 1926, the four-seater Moon Cabriolet I was so attached to."

"Why do you mention that?"

"Because at the time that car meant the world to me. How unhappy it made me when I had to sell it two years later, to finance the soundtrack on *Steamboat Willie*."

"I'm afraid I don't see the connection."

"Your kaleidoscope is worth more to me than my lost Moon Cabriolet. There, is that so hard?"

He asked Hazel to pick him up in the evening and drive him to Anaheim. He wanted to visit his little apartment, and spend the night there with her. She told him he mustn't leave the hospital.

"*I can* . . . of course I can! And on my birthday, and all."

"Silverstein won't allow it."

"I'll be there with you, my love! Just the two of us!"

"Do you want me to ask?"

"No need for that. What I say, goes."

"Soon, in a couple of days, that's a promise."

"Today!"

"A moment ago, you know, you scared me."

"How?"

She changed the subject: "I spy with my little eye, something beginning with T."

"I don't feel like that today, Hazel."

"What do you feel like, then?"

"Rue de Vaugirard."

"What game is that, Walt?"

"It's the Paris game!"

"I don't know what you're talking about."

"Take the Rue de Seine down to the end, and then hang a right on to the Quai de Conti. Cross the Pont Neuf into the first arrondissement."

"I've never been to Paris, Walt."

"Boulevard Sebastopol. And then you could reply: Rue du Temple. But the score would still be one to nothing, my favor, because the Rue du Temple runs parallel to Sebastopol, it's not a cross street. It's only the cross streets that count, you see? Rambuteau would have been right. And then I would have said Temple, and you could have said Place de la Republique. You're allowed to say the squares, even though they don't meet at right angles."

"I'm sorry."

"Can we play now?"

"Walt, why don't you rest a little."

"I don't need to rest."

"I'll get hold of a street map of Paris. I'll try learning it by heart. Then we can play your game. That's a promise."

"Paris! How I love that name! Paris! Will you say it again for me, please, Hazel, Paris! Can you imagine what that was like for me, as a seventeen-year-old greenhorn: I was desperate to fight in the war, I wanted to go after Roy, who was standing in the trenches and shooting at Germans, I wanted to fight like he was! They wouldn't let me. Said I was too young. So I faked the date of birth on my birth certificate, and they sent me over to France. Unfortunately, it was too late: World War One had just ended."

"I know the story, Walt, please."

But he didn't hear Hazel. "There was nothing else I could do," he continued, "other than drive trucks for the Red Cross after the war, the length and breadth of the North of France. And the length and breadth of Paris. My father was descended from a French aristocratic family. A Norman officer by the name of De Isney, who took part in the conquest of England in 1066, was an ancestor of Elias's, that's been documented. They used to live in a fishing village, Isigny-sur-Mer. It still exists, I've visited it several times, as a seventeen-year-old and then later I took my family to see it. Isigny's barely any bigger than Marceline, maybe three thousand inhabitants. Showed my family the beaches of Normandy, Isigny is bang in the middle of Utah and Omaha beach, where the First and Fourth U.S. Divisions came ashore. The tanks and ships and amphibious vehicles, jeeps, bombers, and fighters, almost all of them had Mickey or Donald or Pluto or Goofy emblazoned on the cockpit or the hood! And the most important code word for all the American troops who took part in D-Day was Mickey Mouse!"

"Walt! Calm down, please! I'll come and see you again in the evening."

"But back at the end of 1918 through the summer of 1919, I was driving ambulances and white-painted five-ton trucks all through Paris. Loaded with sugar, flour, beans . . . I know every little street. No Paris taxi driver can fool me: I can tell right away when they're trying to trick me. Rue Soufflot leads to the Place du Pantheon. The Rue Valette to the Rue des Ecoles. Nowhere were my films taken so seriously and reviewed so enthusiastically as they were in Paris after the Second World War. The Rue Cardinal Lemoine leads into the Boulevard Saint Germain. There used to be whole rows of movie theaters there one time, just one after the other. The Boulevard Saint Germain crosses the Boulevard Saint Michel, the Boulevard Saint Michel crosses the Rue Gay Lussac, the Gay Lussac goes into . . ."

He had fallen asleep, the kaleidoscope gripped tightly in his right hand. Hazel tiptoed out of the room.

He dreamed of Paris, he dreamed of Normandy. Isigny turned into Marceline. Marceline-sur-Mer, a fishing village. Isigny was in the heart of the American prairie.

They woke him to put him on a fresh IV.

He dreamed of his favorite uncle Ed, whom he called Elf, roaming through the woods and fields around Marceline with him. The little man, always tanned, with a wrinkled face, showed him where the pheasants and wood pigeons had their nests. They caught frogs and grasshoppers, studied them awhile, and let them go. Mice slipped into his sleeves and trouser legs, got lost in them; others found their way into his big pockets, where there were always little crumbs of cheese. He copied bird calls so convincingly that birds of all kinds came and perched on his shoulders. Uncle Elf was the model for Jiminy Cricket in *Pinocchio*. Walt told Ward Kimball all about his uncle's idiosyncrasies—his tramp's clothing, the umbrella he usually carried with him—and Kimball drew it, gave life, color, and voice, to a grasshopper who personified Pinocchio's conscience. Uncle Ed, though, who brought joy to Walt's childhood, was not to see his nephew again after the good years in Marceline. In 1910, he was put in a mental asylum, where he stayed for the rest of his life.

*

On December 9, 1966, Andy Warhol asked for an audience with Walt Disney. He had been staying in Los Angeles for a few days, and had persuaded his friends from New York, the musicians of the Velvet Underground—Lou Reed, Nico, John Cale, Sterling Morrison, and Maureen Tucker—to accompany him out to the West Coast. At the opening of a Roy Lichtenstein show in a small private museum in Beverly Hills, Warhol learned that Disney, whom he had never met, but idolized from childhood, was in the hospital. His gallerist, Margret Strummond, said it wasn't public knowledge, but she had heard from several of Disney's animators that his condition was serious. Although he feared and detested nothing more in the world than hospitals, Warhol had himself driven to Burbank, and asked the young limousine driver to come back for him an hour later.

Unannounced, as was his style, Andy Warhol was about to walk into suite 401, armed with his new Polaroid Land camera, model Swinger, purchased from Woolworth's for nineteen dollars and fifty cents. The nurse, Miss Bowers, was friendly but firm when Andy asked to be allowed in to see Mr. Disney. The patient was not receiving visitors outside his immediate family. She would be happy to take down the name of the visitor, and would let Mr. Disney know that a Mr. Warhol would like to speak to him. She suggested that he also cross the road to the Disney Studios, and leave a message with his personal assistant. Perhaps a meeting might be arranged.

In the Disney office on the first floor, Warhol, for once not accompanied by his usual entourage of associates and hangers-on, met Tommie Wilck and also Roy. He introduced himself in his soft voice. The pop artist had long since reached the early summits of his fame. His series of

Campbell soup cans, Marilyn, Liz, Elvis, and Atomic Bomb were on show in museums and galleries all over the world, as were the Flower Prints.

Roy didn't know who he was.

"I'm an American artist," Andy Warhol explained to Walt Disney's brother. "I was born the same year as Mickey Mouse, in 1928, in Pittsburgh. My parents came from Czechoslovakia. I feel American through and through. I love this country. It's a great country. It's fantastic. I often have the feeling that I'm representing the United States of America in my art, just like Walt. Why do I like ordinary everyday things best? Why, with the help of my huge army of helpers, who have to do exactly what I tell them to, do I keep on portraying the same film actors and pop stars and myself over and over? It's because that's what I know. It's what I grew up with. I have no interest in criticizing America. God, no. And I don't want to show any ugliness in my work either. Anything but that! I think that—like Walt—I'm a pure artist, really *pure*, in the truest meaning of the word."

Roy nodded understandingly, if also with the feeling: What does this fellow want from us? "I'll let my brother know you came to see him."

"I need to speak to him urgently. As soon as possible. I want to make a portrait of him, for my series of American superstars. And I want Mickey Mouse to be part of a project I'm working on, a project called *Myths*."

"Great idea," said Roy, and hoped the stranger would go away. "I'll pass on to Walt everything you've told me. Write your name on this piece of paper here, and I expect that, once my brother's better, you can have your meeting with him. How did you happen to know he was in the hospital, by the way?"

Andy Warhol wrote his name on the piece of paper, added the words "I love you and I love your work!" and left the studio. He had to wait quite some time for his chauffeur, who had allowed himself a late lunch in a coffee shop nearby, to drive up.

Every evening, Walt's secretary brought over the stack of mail for the day; she did so on that Friday as well.

"What's this?" he asked, as he saw the paper with Warhol's name and message on it.

"Some kind of fan. He'd like to paint you," replied Mrs. Wilck.

"*Paint* me? Crazy idea. Well, we can forget about that. What about Josh's parents? Any word from them?"

"No, nothing, Walt. Not a word."

*

On Sunday, December 11, Ub Iwerks paid a visit. He had heard from Ward Kimball that Disney's condition was deteriorating so rapidly that at times it wasn't possible to speak to the boss any more.

"I'm worried to be seeing *you*: am I that bad, then?"

"I was away on your birthday. I wanted to make it up to you."

"Did you bring me a present?" Walt asked, and handed Ub Hazel's kaleidoscope, telling him to look into it and describe what he saw.

Over the past forty-six years no other animator had been as close to Walt as Ubbe Ert Iwerks, born in 1901 in Kansas City, of Dutch parents. (It was Walt who persuaded him to abbreviate his name.) In 1920, the two nineteen-year-olds had joined forces in Kansas City and founded a production company for promotional cartoon films—the Iwerks-Disney-Studio—which soon went bust. The failure of a second attempt in 1922, the small firm Laugh-O-Grams, was partly responsible for Disney's decision to quit Kansas City and move to Hollywood. No sooner had he settled there than he wrote to Ub, asking him to be the chief draftsman in the production of his own first cartoon series, the *Alice Comedies*. At forty dollars a week, Ub was for a while earning more than his boss, and in the early years he was Walt's only animation artist. He alone produced the early Mickey designs, and according to Ward Kimball, Ub was the man who invented the mouse, for which, up until 1946, Walt spoke in his own falsetto voice. Iwerks single-handedly drew all the early Mickey films, *Plane Crazy*, *Gallopin' Goucho*, and *Steamboat Willie*. He was renowned, at the time, for being able to turn out seven hundred drawings a day, while the rest of us, even the most hard-working, could normally only manage seventy or eighty.

"What about my present?" Walt would not let go.

"You'll have that once you're out. It won't fit in here."

"Is it a plane?"

"Let that be a surprise to you."

Ub Iwerks, a tall and sinewy man, very shy, had more devotion to Walt than anyone else who ever worked for him. And yet, from the beginning, their relationship was characterized by quarrels and conflicts. For years, Disney snubbed his best and most productive animator, treated the man to whom he owed his initial breakthrough worse and tormented him more than any of the nine "old men," never mind someone like me. He couldn't stand it that Ub was so much more talented, original, and imaginative than himself, and was afraid his partner might claim celebrity status for himself and draw attention from him. Ub became so bitter at Walt's treatment that in 1930 he left the studio and tried to take other Disney employees with him in setting up his own company. The experiment to strike out on his own was a lamentable failure. His genius only seemed to count when he was working for Disney. Ten years after leaving, repentant, he came back, but their friendship never again had the same intensity as in the early years.

Disney had fallen asleep while his visitor sat on the edge of the bed. When he woke up, he whispered: "Our world ... created with crayons, pencils and ink ... is a better world, isn't it?"

"The idea of you they have in intellectual circles, the notion that you only ever made pleasant things and that your version of the world is rose-tinted, is completely mistaken," replied Iwerks. "All the gloomy scenes in your movies! There is suffering, loss, betrayal, violence, and sexual awakening. What about the absence of the mother in *Snow White*, in *Pinocchio, Bambi, Cinderella*, and all the wicked stepmothers and witches. What about *Fantasia*?! A firework of light and shade, the paradisal and infernal aspects of the world ..."

"Why don't you just tell me, dammit, what your goddamned present is, instead of rattling on like a whacky professor?!"

At the beginning of November, Ub had gone to Hazel for advice regarding what would best please Walt for his sixty-fifth birthday; he followed the instinct of the studio nurse, who suggested having a new station house built for the railway in his garden.

"So you don't want it to be a surprise, then?"

"Please tell me!"

"I did some research into the way Marceline station looked when you were a boy. There's a book out from the Atchison, Topeka & Santa Fe Society that has a small photograph, where you can see the station quite clearly. I had it built for you, on a 1/8th scale. You'll find it waiting for you in the garden when you get out of here."

Tears rolled down Walt's pale, unshaven face. More and more tears, flowing with ever greater abandon, streaming down from Walt's small, pinched shut eyes. For several minutes, neither man spoke.

Then Walt said, "Do you have any idea, you idiot, what you'd be worth now, if thirty-six years ago you hadn't dropped everything and given up your shares in the company?"

Ub cleared his throat, and checked his own feelings. There was nothing he detested more than sentimentality. It continually embarrassed him. This too was an attitude that had caused a lot of trouble between them from the start.

"Your brother was kind enough to work it out for me once."

"Well? And?"

"Seven hundred million dollars."

"You . . . jackass!"

Miss Bowers was standing in the doorway. Ever since he had seen her for the first time in the intensive care unit five weeks before, she had been his favorite nurse. On account of her white uniform, he called her his Snow White.

Iwerks stood up when Miss Bowers came in.

"He's a junior employee of mine," Walt introduced his closest associate to the young woman.

Ub didn't say anything.

As his friend turned to go, Disney mentioned his decision to make the EPCOT project the focus of his attention for the foreseeable future. He asked Ub to get in touch with the city planner and architect Victor Gruen, to whom he wanted to entrust the responsibility for drawing up a blueprint for his futuristic city. He said: "If I had another fifteen years to live . . ."

"Why shouldn't you?"

"Let me finish. If I still had fifteen years ahead of me, I would outdo and improve on and goddamn surpass everything I've managed to do in the past forty!"

And with that, the two men shook hands.

*

On December 13, Walt awoke screaming that he could stand the pain no longer. Diane was instantly at his bedside. She had spent the night at the hospital. She arranged for him to be given a large dose of morphine. It was half an hour before the poison could take effect. Neither Diane nor Sharon nor Lillian had expected such a steady deterioration in his condition. From early November they had believed unswervingly in the miracle of a cure. They failed to bring in any other consultants, aside from Mrs. Disney's long-time personal physician, who saw the gravity of the situation at once, but was not able or prepared to put this into words.

On that Tuesday morning, Diane prayed. Her parents had not given her a religious upbringing. They rarely, if ever, went to church themselves, and had turned their backs on institutional religion since they were teenagers. But they sent Diane to a Catholic school in Hollywood. She spent at least an hour in passionate prayer, she told Hazel George not many days afterward, begging God to spare Walt any more suffering. Or to cure him that same day, restore him to health immediately! Or make his passing easier. "Hear my prayer!" she whispered as she walked up and down the fourth floor corridor. "Please, Jesus Christ, our Heavenly Lord, take pity on my father!"

She went back in to him. He was very deeply asleep. She noticed that he stopped breathing, sometimes for ten or fifteen seconds at a time. That day, he didn't wake at all. Both the team of doctors and the nursing staff expected their patient not to survive the night.

*

The next morning he woke up refreshed. He told the nurses he would like some tea and a small breakfast. Miss Bowers called for Dr. Silverstein. She couldn't believe her eyes or ears. Walt seemed stronger and more alert than at any time since his second hospitalization. Silverstein examined him, and found a distinct stabilization of the circulation and respiratory system. Only in extremely rare cases in a career spanning many years had he witnessed a comparable turn in the overall condition of a gravely ill patient, he told the family. Walt, however, seemed to possess an amazing reservoir of willpower, enabling him to set aside, at least temporarily, the evident hopelessness of his condition. Lillian asked the doctors and her daughters if they would leave her alone with her husband for a while. Only Miss Bowers remained in the room, changing the sheets while Walt sat upright in an armchair.

"Would you mind going out for a moment, please?" asked Mrs. Disney.

"That's OK, Snow White can stay."

Lillian was by no means pleased, but she gave in. "You did it, Walt!" She grasped his hands, kissed him on the forehead. "Now everything's going to be fine."

"Fine . . . I think so. We'd better celebrate."

"You bet we'll celebrate!"

"A trip abroad, just the two of us. An ocean liner! The Italians have just launched a wonderful ship, the Leonardo da Vinci. Goes from Long Beach to Venice, through the Panama Canal!"

"Venice, Florence, maybe Rome, if it's not too much of a strain."

"I want to go to France too!"

"So do I, Walt!"

"We'll spend a whole week in Paris! At the Ritz or the Bristol."

"I prefer the Lutetia."

"The Lutetia it is! Boulevard Raspail, corner of the Rue du Cherche Midi."

*

Roy was overjoyed to find his brother in such good spirits when he came to pay his regular four o'clock visit. No sooner had he sat down on the chair between the bed and the window than Walt pointed up at the white tiles on the ceiling. For over an hour, he used the overhead grid of tiles to plan the various sectors of the utopian social experimental city EPCOT. To his inner eye, the ceiling became a map of the future, a utopia in the true sense of the word: the dreamed, imaginary land, where people would live together in an ideal society.

He asked Roy to fix up a meeting with Ronald Reagan, who in November had been elected governor of California, and whose gubernatorial term was to commence in January. He wanted to discuss possible ways of improving the quality of life in the state, ideas he wanted to put to him concerning first and foremost the traffic in and around Los Angeles. If the car industry were simply allowed to grow—here he was of one mind with his friend and admirer Ray Bradbury—then in a matter of a few decades the whole of Southern California would be a network of freeways. The cause of public transportation had to be promoted, ideally a monorail system of the kind that was already up and running in the Tomorrowland of Anaheim. Walt insisted he wanted to speak to the governor-elect before Christmas. Roy promised he would get in touch with him immediately.

"Our friend could even become president one day," Walt predicted to his brother. "There's nothing to prevent it. Anything's possible!"

"Walt, he's an actor . . ."

"He's a statesman, Roy, trust me, I have an instinct for things like that."

When, for the first time during the weeks of his two stays at St. Joseph's, Walt heard the cry of a screech owl outside the hospital in the early evening, he took it as a further sign of the rapid improvement of his condition.

*

Before Hazel George met me, the relationship she had with Miss Bowers, dominated by a passionate shared interest in Walt and his life, in some ways prefigured the one she would have with me. She made the nurse the present of a bottle of Fleurs de Rocaille, and brought books, records, and comics from the Disney Studios opposite, because Snow White had a large gang of nieces and nephews to provide with Christmas presents. It was from Miss Bowers that Hazel found out everything she wanted to know about Walt's second stay at the hospital, including the events of December 15, an unusually gray day for Los Angeles. It was cool, and though it rained off and on, a dense, orange smog hung over the largest city in the world.

Miss Bowers went on duty at six o'clock that Thursday morning. When she entered Walt's room, expecting to find him feeling as well, if not better, than he had felt the day before, she noticed that his pulse was beating very rapidly. She spoke to him.

He opened his eyelids, let them fall shut, and muttered, with eyes closed: "There's only one thing that matters to me. I want them to remember me as a *storyteller* . . ."

Miss Bowers noted Walt's extreme breathlessness. She rang for the doctor on duty, Jack Carlson, because Silverstein wouldn't be in before nine o'clock. While waiting for Carlson, she held Walt's hand, which felt very cold.

"I'm terribly, terribly, terribly scared, Snow White," he whispered.

She tried to calm him.

"I'm so . . . so scared!" he said again.

Miss Bowers wondered whether she should go to wake Sharon, who was asleep on the same floor of the hospital, but she felt she couldn't leave Walt on his own even for a second.

"Snow White . . . I'm so frightened of dying . . ."

"It'll be all right, don't worry, sir."

"Don't . . . call me . . . sir . . ."

The doctor's footsteps could be heard as he ran along the corridor, followed by his assistant.

"It's a fact," whispered Walt, "only the fittest . . . prevail. . . . Nothing to be done about that!"

Carlson rushed in. An oxygen tank was wheeled in, the patient hooked up to an ECG and equipment to stabilize his circulation. The circulation was very uneven, now far too high, now far too low. The doctor instructed Miss Bowers to summon Sharon.

When Mrs. Brown set foot in suite 401, at eight o'clock, she was informed that her father's condition had declined in the course of the last few hours. She ran back to her room, beside herself with pain and shock. Only the night before, her father had seemed to be making a rapid recovery. In tears she called her mother, her sister, and her uncle.

Silverstein arrived shortly before nine, and ordered the patient to be taken immediately to the operating room. There, a team of four doctors did everything that was technically and medically possible in December 1966, to restore the patient's collapsing circulation.

At nine thirty-five a.m., Walt Disney stopped breathing.

*

I was there in the early evening of December 15, when the plain wooden coffin was carried out of St. Joseph's and lifted into a hearse. There were several onlookers—the midday radio and television news had announced Walt's passing—but nobody stayed behind on Buena Vista Street as long as I did. When the funeral home's Cadillac drove off, I got into my car and followed it. After fifteen minutes on the freeway, the black limousine reached the Glendale exit, and turned into Forest Lawn Memorial Park, which was also open to private vehicles. The hearse parked outside an administration building, and then the coffin was carried inside by four men.

Glendale, southeast of Burbank, west of Pasadena, is about ten miles north of downtown Los Angeles. Train tracks go past the cemetery, which isn't far from the station that Billy Wilder made such effective use of in *Double Indemnity*. Its extensive lawns are so green, its trees so artfully arranged on landscaped hills, that it makes you think of a golf course more than a final resting place. Clark Gable and Carole Lombard are buried here, Jean Harlow and Clara Bow, and Erroll Flynn, of whom the story goes that he was buried with half a dozen bottles of bourbon, at the end of October in the year of my dismissal, 1959.

I took a room in the two-story Howard Johnson's right across from the main entrance to the cemetery, so as to be able to keep it under surveillance and not to miss the moment of the funeral. The night was even worse than my nights usually were. I kept getting up, going over to the window, looking out at the freeway and the railroad tracks. Freight trains were shunted this way and that. The squeal of their brakes, the jangle and clunk of their bumpers, the shrill of their warning whistles pierced my hearing. I could make out the outlines of the cemetery walls. Within me there was nothing but dread and horror. Goosebumps all over my body. Took myself back to bed. Saw my life as a condemned building, no single room, no wall intact. I left the hotel for a twenty-four-hour liquor store to get a bottle of Cutty Sark, Walt's favorite whiskey in his last years, as Ward Kimball had told me. Back in my room, I forced myself to down the firewater, but managed no more than a third of the bottle. I smoked a small joint with it. Nothing helped. Not until the early light fell across the large double bed did I manage to get a couple of hours of sleep.

At half past ten in the morning, I went to the administration building and saw Roy talking to a group of cemetery employees. From his clothes, a set of tails, a bowler hat, and a black bow tie, I concluded that the funeral might take place this very Friday, the day after Walt's death. Jews and Muslims bury their dead as soon as possible. But with us Christians, don't people usually wait a week or even ten days before the funeral?

As soon as Roy Disney had disappeared into the cemetery office, I went up to one of the men who were standing around outside the front door. I said I was a relative of Walt Disney's: "Excuse me, am I too early for Walt's funeral?" I asked the plump, rosy-cheeked Forest Lawn employee.

The event was scheduled for three in the afternoon, but my informant had been told not to pass on any information about it; he could only hope I was indeed related as I claimed to be, otherwise his job would be at risk.

"What is your job, if I might ask?"

"I'm the man," he laughed proudly, "who pushes the button and makes the fire come on."

I didn't understand. "Is my Walt then . . . is he not being buried?"

"Of course not."

"Oh?"

"Cremated, didn't they tell you?"

I had no idea at the time that Walt's last wish had been his cryo-biological preservation. It wasn't until some weeks later that I met Dr. Silverstein and Hazel George. Even so, the idea that his mortal remains were to be incinerated seemed to me to be completely at odds with my sense of the man.

"Are you sure about that?" I ventured to ask.

"Hundred percent, my friend. And now, will you please excuse me."
He turned and vanished into the building, along with his grinning
colleagues.

Not only was I surprised that Walt was to be cremated, I was also
astonished at the haste of the proceedings. I wondered whether I should
try to get in touch with Ward Kimball or Ub Iwerks, John Lounsbery or
Wolfgang Reitherman, those four studio men I still felt close to. I promptly
rejected the idea again, not least because I liked being the only outsider to
know where and when the boss was to receive his final honors.

*

Walt Disney was committed to the flames on Friday, December 16, at
three thirty in the afternoon, in the small, Tuscan-style crematorium in
Glendale cemetery. I stood behind the half-open chapel door, and listened to the Hammond organ playing the tune "Feed the Birds" from
Mary Poppins, Walt's favorite piece of music from the latter years. I
watched the black smoke pour out of the chimney. And then, when the
family moved on to the place where the urn was to be deposited, I trailed
after them at a distance of fifty or sixty feet. I was not the only person
standing around. There were various anonymous visitors in the cemetery,
but I was the only one to know who the little group of mourners really
were. There was no one but Walt's closest relatives in attendance, I
counted ten of them. Once again, the family had kept to itself.

None of the grandchildren were permitted to witness their grandfather's cremation. Ruth, his youngest sister, wasn't there either; she
hadn't managed to get down from Portland in time. Herbert, the oldest,
had been dead for five years. Walt had refused to attend the funeral. (On
the few occasions when he did go to burials, he would fall into days, even
weeks, of depression.) Walt's next oldest brother, Raymond, an insurance
salesman in Hollywood, who was born in 1890, and whom I saw on that

day for the first and last time, accompanied his nieces and in-laws. He was wearing a dinner jacket that didn't fit him. His crooked walk and large, clumsy body reminded me a little of the French film director Jacques Tati.

I watched as Diane carried the urn, in theatrically outstretched arms, flanked by Lillian and Roy's wife Edna, both in black veils. Sharon and her husband, Bob Brown, and Diane's husband, Ron Miller also escorted Walt's only biological daughter. Roy stayed a few steps behind the others. After ten minutes they reached the foot of a knoll of grass, where they deposited the urn of ashes in an improvised niche in a wall.

I turned away, and left the family behind me. I walked back toward my hotel, feeling absolutely shattered. Muggy afternoon heat lay over Glendale. "I'm more famous than Confucius or the Queen of England," I heard Walt's voice in my head. "More people know my name than the name of William Shakespeare, Mark Twain, or Adolf Hitler."

CHAPTER NINE

In the days and weeks following his death, I scoured every newspaper and magazine I could possibly find, looking for the least little article about the deceased. I kept everything—every obituary, every essay, everything that came into my hands that had to do with Walt Disney. And not just American publications: I also had things sent to me from Europe. I studied French, Italian, and German papers, and asked my father's Puerto Rican housekeeper to translate items that had appeared in Latin America or Spain.

In the news magazine *Paris Match*, I came upon a statement from a prominent French doctor highly critical of his colleague Dr. Silverstein. A whole string of poor decisions had, in his opinion, hastened Disney's death. Robert David Calvo, senior surgeon at the Necker Hospital in Paris, stated that he would certainly not have operated right away in the case of a patient with a small lung tumor, but would have offered him radiation therapy. What had been especially irresponsible was allowing Disney to leave the hospital only two weeks after the removal of an entire lung. Anyone undergoing an operation of such magnitude needed at least five weeks of supervised care afterward, and ideally six or eight.

At the end of January 1967, Ward Kimball was invited to an evening given by Disney's doctor for close friends and associates of the deceased.

I asked my former colleague if he would take me. Dr. Silverstein's villa in Beverly Canyon was not far from Walt's property in Holmby Hills. I've mentioned it already: it was on this occasion that I first made the acquaintance of Hazel George. I told her quite a bit about myself on that very first evening, but was careful to divulge nothing of my secret obsession with her employer, for whom she was in deep mourning.

I have no intention of attacking Silverstein in the way that Calvo did, but I can't avoid saying that I was not overly impressed with Walt's surgeon. Roy, Lillian, Diane, and Sharon did not have their brother, husband, and father, respectively, treated by the best physicians in the country, but were happy to use the services of a man who happened to be across the road from the studios—without consulting anyone else. At that time, the mid-sixties, Boston and Chicago had the most advanced cancer clinics in America, if not the whole world. The Sloan-Kettering Institute in New York was breaking new ground. Why was Walt Disney, one of the richest and most powerful men in the U.S.A., never taken to one of these specialist clinics; alternatively, why was no doctor from one of these three cities flown to Los Angeles?

The little group of twenty or so of those present was informed by Silverstein that it had been Disney's last wish that his body be frozen. To me, this news sounded like an artificial cornerstone of a modern myth, but both the surgeon and Hazel George went on to speak of the progress and possibilities of cryobiology with such certainty and conviction that it seemed that the storing of Walt's anatomical remains in liquid nitrogen would have been a perfectly natural, almost straightforward matter, if only the family had agreed with Walt's clearly stated desire. But no sooner had Disney passed away, on the morning of December 15, than Roy and Lillian set everything in motion for his immediate incineration.

"Mrs. Disney referred to Walt's wishes as childish lunacy," Silverstein reported to the guests. "I pointed out that her husband had expressly asked me to subject him to this novel mode of 'burial.' Moreover, I had promised it to him, on the 'Old Testament,' as he referred to my Bible, the Torah."

"And I had to swear on the flag of the United States of America," Hazel added.

I couldn't help but laugh, and my sacrilegious outburst earned me a few dirty looks. With the tip of his boot, Ward kicked me under the table.

"Hazel having asked me," Dr. Silverstein carried on, "once more to do everything in my power to see to it that Walt's most fervently held desire was put into effect, I had a conversation with Roy at about noon on Friday the 15th. It was no use: He would hardly listen to me, and just kept shaking his head. The family had made up their minds. Against their opposition, there was nothing that Hazel and I could do."

Over the years and decades since Walt's passing, reports that Walt's body was in cold storage in Disneyland, in Anaheim, deep under the Pirates of the Caribbean, or in some secret location elsewhere, in order to be thawed out at some future date, have continued to circulate to the point that they are widely believed in many parts of the world.

*

In 1967 and 1968, I devoted myself almost entirely to the painstaking exploration of Walt's biography in its every nuance and detail. Were it not for Hazel's help and support, for which I should like to thank her publicly at this point, this task would certainly have been insurmountable.

From spring of 1967 on, Hazel and Ward Kimball kept insisting: Wilhelm Dantine, you must make something of your life! You mustn't give all your remaining years solely and exclusively to Walt Disney. Otherwise you'll end up just like the magnificent animator Norm Ferguson, the creator of Pluto, fired by Walt in 1953, and dead of a coronary a few years later—"died of a broken heart," we all said at the time. And what are you going to live on? Your father's money, when he's not even all that well off? Is your only reason for living to keep the memory of your beloved antagonist alive, nothing else? It still took me well over a year to begin to pay some heed to the drumming of these enviably supportive friends of mine. And if my thoughts and dreams still remained caught up with Walt, even after 1968, then—thanks to the encouragement of Ward Kimball and Hazel George—I did at least succeed in finding work that was reasonably fulfilling.

I could have gotten a job as an animator for most any other studio. But that didn't fit the sort of self-image I'd mapped out for myself. I felt I had to keep being sincerely faithful to my archenemy and idol, even past his death. I needed to continue to feel the pain of having lost Walt. My new line of work allowed me to keep alive a fascination that had been with me since childhood: the analysis of movement in twenty-four frames per second—tracking the enigma we call "the second" with the help of moving sequences. And hence to voyage into time, to split it up into its constituent atoms. I became a cameraman.

Through Ward Kimball's agency, I met the cameraman Wolf Suschitzky, born in Vienna in 1912, and living in England since 1938, and studied with him for a year, initially as his second assistant and grader during the filming of *Ulysses*, directed by Joseph Strick after James Joyce's original.

On his very next project, *Ring of Bright Water*, Suschitzky promoted me to first assistant. Strick was once again the director, and the narrative, about a writer who buys himself an otter in London and withdraws into nature with it, could hardly have been more Disneyesque. The film was seen as a modern myth, a film for animal lovers, of the kind that previously it would have taken Walt to produce.

My new master handed me on to his son Peter, who, from the mid-sixties on, was also working as a cameraman. I assisted him on *Lock Up Your Daughters*, a piece of nonsense set in eighteenth-century London. The filming did have the one benefit for me that I got to meet the actress Glynis Johns, who in *Mary Poppins* had played Winifred, the mother of Jane and Michael Banks. We used every lunch break, every interval in the filming, to talk about Walt. And nothing else. It was Glynis who told me that the original choice to play the role of the flying nanny had been Bette Davis, and the only reason she didn't get the part was that Disney didn't like her singing voice. And she described the film's premiere in 1964, at Grauman's Chinese Theater, on Hollywood Boulevard. No sooner had the curtain come down, and Walt left the stage after taking his bows, than Mrs. Travers, the author of the stories the film had been based on, a stern old lady, came storming toward him. "You have made a mockery of my work!" she scolded, waving her fists in the direction of the cast who stood together at the foot of the stage. "The film cannot possibly stay as it is. It will not be released in that form! I protest! What are those songs doing in my story? And those ridiculous dance sequences?! When can we start re-editing?" It had taken weeks for Walt to get the irate authoress to understand the unpalatable truth: that with the sale of the rights to her books, she had given up any say in the adaptation.

In the early seventies, I made my only documentary film to date. I was cameraman, writer, director, and producer of a forty-five minute portrait of Ward Kimball made for the BBC. I managed to get my old friend to admit, on camera, that in fact it was he alone who was responsible for the 1941 cartoon film *Dumbo*, the story of a baby elephant whose enormous ears enable him to soar through the air like an eagle. It was Ward's idea, and he was co-director with Ben Sharpsteen. He was the main artist on this worldwide hit, and then Walt Disney came along and pocketed all the awards and prizes, as well as profits running into millions of dollars. All Walt had done was to approve the project before running off to South America, to get away as far as possible from the ongoing cartoonists' strike and its consequences.

I filmed Ward in his garden in the San Gabriel Valley, in the caboose of his steam locomotive, a 1907 Baldwin, which pulled passenger and freight cars on a circuit of his Grizzly Flats Railroad. Ward was another railroad freak, and he admitted, also on camera, that he had been the one to give Walt the idea of setting up a model railway on his property in Holmby Hills.

My film showed the remarkable extent to which even one of the most gifted and creative members of the Burbank Studios crew was prepared to withdraw into the shadows and allow Walt Disney's name to stand alone. Ward told me he had worked over three hours on a single drawing of Bacchus for *Fantasia*, and that one second of Bacchic dancing on film had taken him a week. And for all that, he still felt that Walt was the creator of *Fantasia*, not himself or the large support team. His basic message was: "No one I ever met had such a gift for stimulating and motivating others as he did. He had a positively uncanny feeling for a man's creative potential—and then forced him to really produce it where it mattered. Extraordinary. Incomparable." But then again, Victor Gruen had spoken in similar terms about Walt, as had Heinz Haber, Glynis Johns, Peter Ustinov, Chuck Amen, and all the other acquaintances and associates of his that I was to meet over the years.

"What about a critical word you'd like to get off your chest to end with?" I tried to lure Kimball out of his reserve.

"People still know the name of Leonardo four hundred and fifty years after his death, and the same goes for Michelangelo, and Rubens, and Velázquez," he replied. "Disney will have the same standing long into the future. And that's the way it should be. Walt's films may be simplifications, but they are still classics. They ought to be preserved, no, they *will* be preserved in the same way that people preserved the Gutenberg Bible."

In the following years, I mostly worked as a cameraman, and sometimes as an assistant. I was also a focus-puller, that member of the camera team who has the not-to-be-underestimated job of seeing that the lens is correctly adjusted during a shot. I traveled a lot in the seventies and eighties, but kept L.A. as my base. From 1974 on, I rented a little guest house on the property of the blues musician, John Mayall, on Oakstone Way, in the Hollywood Hills. I took advantage of my frequent absences on the road, while doing my job, to continue to pursue my interest in Walt's story, and my quest for what was at the core of his personality.

Of all the various directors and cameramen I worked under, no one gave me a comparable feeling of intimidation, awe, and contempt to what I had had for Walt Disney. By comparison, they all seemed shallow, mediocre, passionless. With perhaps one exception, one half-exception: during the filming of Wim Wenders's film *Paris, Texas*, in the spring of 1984, the Dutch-born cinematographer and lighting artist Robby Müller struck me as being spiritually ablaze. Robby became a friend of mine, and he still is today. It was he who brought me together with Jim Jarmusch, and the three of us worked on *Mystery Train* together, a dreamy, episodic film about four somnambulist protagonists who all idolized the late Elvis Presley.

*

The same afternoon that Geraldine Chaplin agreed to show me a shoebox full of letters that she kept in her bedroom in Vevey, Pope John Paul II was shot in St. Peter's Square in Rome. We sat on her bed, on May 13, 1981, watching the news on Swiss television. The live reports gave the impression that the pontiff, though badly wounded, was conscious, and about to undergo an emergency operation.

Geraldine, whose mother had been a friend of my mother's, treated me like a long-lost cousin on the few occasions that we saw each other. A family legend has it that Chaplin had been introduced to his subsequent wife Oona O'Neill, then just seventeen, by my mother—in Musso & Frank's restaurant, Walt's former haunt, and also Chaplin's favorite eaterie on Hollywood Boulevard.

One of my early childhood memories is indirectly bound up with Geraldine. My mother used to take me along with her to Oona's house quite often, and one of these visits seems to stand out from the rest. I was eight years old. Oona was having trouble breathing, and she asked me to lay my head on her belly. I was very shy, but mother and Mrs. Chaplin, just eighteen, as I now know, encouraged me. Hesitantly I clambered up on to Charlie Chaplin's wide matrimonial bed, and pressed my head against the belly of the heavily pregnant Oona. I felt, on my temples and on my cheeks, the little hand movement and kicks of the unborn infant. When Geraldine was born, in July 1944, I went with Mother to the hospital in Santa Monica, and counted the many vases of flowers spilling out of Oona's room and on into the hall. I had last seen Geraldine when she was fourteen, on the occasion of one of our rare visits back to Europe. She was living with her parents then, in the same villa as now, when I came to visit in May 1981, in Vevey, on Lake Geneva. (I had gone there with Alain Resnais, who was making preparations for his film, *La Vie Est un Roman*. He was thinking of using me as his cameraman, and was meeting Geraldine to try to convince her to take on the lead role.)

In the black Prada shoebox that Miss Chaplin handed me were letters to her father that she especially treasured. "The reason I like them so much and want to keep them," she told me, "is that they have a different tone from most of the letters Daddy got." After some initial hesitation, she agreed to leave the box with me for a couple of hours. I ordered a taxi and rode to the nearest photocopying shop, and had it wait while I ran off postcards, letters, and telegrams.

With my belly pressed against the overheating machine, I stopped to read one particular letter to Mr. Charles Spencer Chaplin very carefully. It was from 1946 and made me oddly happy. My mother wrote requesting that he be discreet about their meetings in the past, especially with Oona. Having been rather unsuspecting, she was now worried that my father would hear of her little adventure. I had always been very eager to meet Mr. Chaplin, but Mother had always arranged to see Oona when Charlie happened to be away filming or in some other way unavailable. Only now, seventeen years after her death, did I understand.

Franklin D. Roosevelt sent his idol a congratulatory telegram on his fiftieth birthday, on April 16, 1939: "YOUR NAME WILL OUTLAST MINE IN HISTORY," it read, signed, "Sincerely, FDR." Thomas Mann had sent a postcard, dated November 19, 1940: "Dear, esteemed Mr. Chaplin, saw your dictator film yesterday. Very charming, perhaps somewhat too nonsensical farce and parody, with numerous comic touches that made me laugh a good deal. I hope to see you soon. Respectfully yours, TM."

And then I came upon a copy of the airmail letter that I was to read many, many times that night in my Geneva hotel room. I still know every word of it by heart. It left Holmby Hills on October 11, 1966, two days after my thirtieth birthday: "Dear Chaplin, I've owed you an apology for fourteen years now, ever since you left America. What I did and said cannot be made good. I know you will not be able to forgive me. I would only like you to know how much you mean to me. Without your example, there would have been no Mickey Mouse. Without your inspiration, there would have been no *Snow White* or *Pinocchio* or indeed the great majority of my films. You were my teacher and my idol. Without you, there would have been no Walt Disney. I embrace you. Yours sincerely, Walt Disney."

When I said good-bye to Geraldine the next morning (the news was full of the Pope's remarkable recovery following an emergency operation), I asked Miss Chaplin whether she had ever met Walt in person. She passed the back of her hand across her narrow, bony face, which on that day looked strikingly pale, almost sickly, and pulled on a cardigan. She felt the cold. The room was very large, and the stone-flagged floors gave out a damp chill.

"I saw him only once," she then said. "It was in the Palace Hotel Des Bains, on the Lido in Venice, during the film festival. Daddy was the guest of honor, and received a Lion d'Or for his lifetime's achievement. I was sixteen or seventeen at the time. Disney was pacing up and down in the hotel lobby, probably waiting for his wife, nobody knew who he was. A tall and graceful figure, slightly stooped, with beautiful hands and long, elegant fingers that rested for a moment on one of the big lobby armchairs. He was holding a cigarette, and the ash fell on the damask. I passed him, very close, like a cat, and studied him as closely as I could. He struck me as warm, attractive, and kind. All things that didn't really fit the picture of him I had from my father, all the years I was growing up. You must remember that as a child I never, ever got to see his films. Never held a Mickey Mouse comic book in my hands. Had barely heard of Donald Duck. Only since father's death, three years ago, have I started to get to know his work. And now that you can get everything on video, I can buy all his classic films." To date, she owned only one, *The Jungle Book*. And she wouldn't allow her little son to watch it, at least not yet.

*

The Jungle Book was released in the fall of 1967, nine months after Walt's death. For the family, the huge, worldwide success of the last work to which Disney had still made some personal contribution (admittedly, probably the least of any of the cartoon films, with the exception of *Dumbo*) coincided with more grief: Sharon's husband, Bob Brown, died on September 13, 1967, of lung cancer, at the age of thirty-nine. He too was cremated, and his urn was laid to rest directly below Walt's, in Forest Lawn Memorial Park. Sharon also died of lung cancer, in 1993, just fifty-six.

Roy died of a stroke on December 20, 1971, two months after the moment he had worked toward for eight years solidly—the last five of them with redoubled intensity—the opening of Disney World, just outside Orlando, Florida. EPCOT was never realized in the form in which Walt and Victor Gruen dreamed. From the early eighties, there has been a theme park called EPCOT, but that is no more than a small exhibition on the theme of global technological progress, and has nothing in common with the original utopian conception of EPCOT but the name.

A few years ago, I attended Hazel George's funeral in her native New Florence, Montana. She had started living there again in the mid-eighties. It was snowing hard as we carried her to her grave, the little group of friends and relatives who were all she had left. Walt hadn't mentioned her in his updated will of November 1966, and I think that made my friend rather bitter, even though she would never admit it to me. All she asked for in the way of mementoes of her boss were the kaleidoscope and the Indian wool rug. The family immediately agreed to let her have those things.

In July 1991, in the course of a short visit to his birthplace, my father, Egon Philipp Dantine, suffered a massive heart attack in his room in the Hotel Römischer Kaiser. I arranged for him to be buried in the Central Cemetery in Vienna. A year later, I was back there, this time to bury my sister, Marika, in the same grave. (Mother is lying in Los Angeles, in a small cemetery in the San Fernando Valley. I have left instructions for my body to be interred next to hers, and on no account next to those of my father and sister.)

*

On the morning of my sixtieth birthday, October 9, 1996, thirty years after I invaded the garden of the villa in Holmby Hills with my son Jonathan, I visited the cemetery in Glendale for the first time since December 16, 1966. It was nine o'clock, and the gate had only just opened. I easily found my way back to the spot where I had stood then. A modest plaque had been put up in a brick wall, over a dark gray steel plate. Vertically ranked were the names of Walter Elias Disney, Robert B. Brown, and Sharon Disney Brown. Behind the metal plate, I assumed, were the embrasures holding the individual urns.

I could see no one around, with the exception of an old gardener in pale green uniform, who was driving along a ridge in the sort of tiny motorized cart that golfers use.

The top metal plate was slightly bent back on the left. I touched its razor-sharp edge. I thought I would push it back into place. Instead I did the opposite, and tugged at the steel. It took considerable exertion and not a little skill on my part, but I managed to pull it out further and further, until I had torn off the entire upper plate. I couldn't believe what I was doing. On my sixtieth birthday, I was behaving like an eighteen-year-old vandal. I reached into the open compartment, felt cold air brush my hand. And touched the urn, pulled it out, was surprised at its weight. I held Walt's urn in my hands, an ugly, grayish-black thing, stamped with "W.E.D., Dec. 5, 1901–Dec. 15, 1966." I tried for two or three minutes to reattach the plate, and then gave up.

I don't remember very well what I did next, even though it happened only six months ago. I took off my jacket, wrapped it round the urn, and went back to the empty parking lot where I'd left my car. I took the Pasadena Freeway East and drove east for a long time, until the first streaks of evening appeared in the rearview mirror. I had a midnight-blue Mercedes Coupé that looked very like the model that Walt drove at the end of his life. I stopped at a gas station, and—this too I only know because I was told about it afterward—called my ex-wife Martha. I told her that the little party she'd organized for my birthday, to which Ward Kimball and his family had also been invited, would have to go on without me. Something had come up. She burst into tears, asked me where I was, and if I wasn't doing something stupid, because my voice sounded so strange and distant. Subsequent reconstruction of events confirms that I was calling from a Shell station in Globe, Arizona.

The journey from Southern California to Missouri took four days. I reached Marceline on the afternoon of Saturday, October 13. From the moment I reached Walt's boyhood home, my memory is almost completely intact. In a garden equipment store next to Murray's clothes shop on what was still called Kansas Avenue, I bought myself a blood-red shovel. Not a big one with a long handle, more the kind of thing you use to plant rose bushes.

I felt like I was in a dream. The old movie house, the fire station, the barbershop, the town hall, the candy store—they were all completely unchanged, just the way they were when I had seen them thirty years before. The train station, too, was untouched, even though no freight or passenger trains had stopped there for quite some years. The entrance was behind heavy iron chains. The defining sound of the place was still the thundering of the passing trains, the long low whistle of the locomotives. It was as though Marceline was dozing in a hundred-year sleep, and the handful of people I saw there looked to me distinctly like sleep-walkers. They didn't nod, they didn't say hello, they didn't see me, and they seemed to look through and past each other as well.

I found my way back to the farm that, ninety years ago, had been Walt's home, and it too looked the way I remembered it. The remarkably tall, steep roof. The wide, pretty porch. The two low stories. The red paint was flaking here and there, but apart from that nothing seemed to have changed. I parked my car on Broadway, right by the Disneys' farm, just where Mrs. Murray had shown me Walt's favorite tree in September 1966, the one she called the "belly-button tree." I sat in the car and smoked a joint. I used up the last of the grass I had on me. Then I got out.

It started to drizzle. The elm looked taller and bushier to me since last time. It must have grown a lot. Its trunk felt like elephant skin grown over dinosaur bones. Its leaves had taken on all the colors of fall. Crows flew round the tree, cawed so loud it was like they were calling to all the other crows in the state of Missouri. A little breeze sprang up. I knelt down next to the belly-button tree, and started digging a hole with the shovel. I cut through threads of roots, hit against stones, wrecked beetle caves, and found a grime-rusted cent from the year 1952, which I put in my pocket. I dug on deeper and faster now, until I could get my arm in the hole up to the elbow. I went over to the car and got out the urn that had been on the backseat under my jacket for the last few days. It seemed even heavier now than when I had pulled it out of its embrasure. I tried to lower the urn with Walt Disney's remains into the hole. It was too narrow. I scraped away mani-cally, until the shovel's handle broke off, widened the opening as best I could, and finally stuffed the iron urn into its farm-earth grave, covered it up, and scraped topsoil, twigs, and leaves over it.

"What are you doing there?" A woman's voice, right beside me.

I turned round. A friendly face bent down over me.

"I live here," said the woman. "You're on my property. What are you doing, digging here? What are you looking for?"

I didn't know what to reply. She had pale blue eyes I liked. Short blond hair. She looked like she must be in her mid-forties. I got up slowly, whispered: "I'm sorry."

"What are you sorry about?"

"For trespassing on your property."

"I'm going to call the police."

"Please don't do that. I can explain everything."

"You'd better."

I didn't say anything.

She took out a cell phone, punched seven digits. "Hi. This is Kaye. Kaye Malins, that's right: 100 Broadway, corner of North Missouri Street. Could you send a car right away? I've got someone on my property. Thanks."

"You didn't have to do that," I heard myself mutter.

"Well, what are you doing here? Can't you see the fence marking off the garden from the street?"

"I'm sorry."

"I'm sorry, too. You don't look like a criminal."

Marceline, Missouri's one patrol car arrived a few minutes later. Rather needlessly, the siren had been turned on, which only drove up my adrenaline level a point or two. I was bundled into the backseat by two policemen, and driven to the police station, which was right next to the railway station. Beside the single platform, I spotted an old, decaying wooden sign that read: "Walt Disney's Boyhood Home Marceline Missouri Welcomes You."

It didn't take long for the sheriff and his deputy to get a confession out of me. After a few minutes of silence, I admitted everything, at least everything I could remember. The Marceline police computer, which logged into the World Wide Web, promptly brought up my 1966 arrest. I was fingerprinted, and allowed to make my one telephone call. I called Martha. She had sensed that something was wrong. I asked her to find me a lawyer to post bail and represent me at the subsequent hearing.

I had to spend two nights in the single cell in the Marceline police station. On the little television set fitted on a short metal arm high above my bed, the evening news on the Macon-based station KNC-TV showed the belly-button tree in all its glory; they also ran a short interview with Kaye Malins. The report said that the urn containing Walt Disney's ashes, which had disappeared on October 9, had showed up in his childhood home of Marceline, Missouri. The "emotionally unstable urn-napper" was a former employee of the Burbank Studios, whom Walt Disney had fired in late 1959. At the end of the report, it added that the man was now in police custody.

*

On Monday, October 15, 1996, I was transferred to St. Louis. My car was impounded. A Justice Department minibus took me to the central penitentiary of the state of Missouri. I decided not to post bail, as I was assured the case against me could be brought as early as the following week. The attorney Martha found me was no match for the judge, nor did he have the least understanding of his client's previous history or subsequent path. In fact, I couldn't have found a more inept or uninterested attorney than Dr. Martin Perry, my ex-wife's brother-in-law, if I'd tried. And, strange as it may seem, it didn't bother me at all to lose the case. Since there was no jury and only a handful of witnesses, the entire hearing was over in two and a half hours. One of the witnesses, incidentally, was Edgar Murray, Eileen's son, who now owned the clothes shop. He remembered my turning up thirty years before, described my curious behavior to the judge. Putting two and two together, Edgar concluded that I had intended to assassinate Walt Disney on that day in September when the swimming pool was dedicated. Moments after giving his testimony against me, Edgar walked up to me during a break in the proceedings, and greeted me as if I was an old friend of his. His mother, he said, had died in May 1972. His only son,

Michael, winner of several statewide angling contests, had joined the Marines, and was presently stationed in Saudi Arabia.

The sentence didn't surprise me: four months. My attorney and I had both expected a stiffer punishment, I thought six months, Dr. Perry a year. The fact that I had a conviction from 1967 for possession of marijuana (my visit to the garden in Holmby Hills didn't appear in any files) made my misdemeanor, Judge James Hutchinson declared, far graver. Had I not had a police record, I would certainly have got away with a suspended sentence. Hutchinson gave me the impression he was sorry about my impending loss of liberty. He had no way of knowing that I was perfectly reconciled to my punishment. I asked the court if I might do my time in solitary confinement. The court psychiatrist, Dr. Chris Morris-Bertell, who had served as an expert witness, helped me to get my wish. In large part because of his gracious and unobtrusive support and his wise initiative, between November 1996 and March 1997 I was able to complete the first draft of the present manuscript at the Missouri State Penitentiary in St. Louis.

Being given four months in which to write, without any distraction, housed in a small cell (I had always preferred small studies, even when I was a boy), with no rent, no electricity, phone, or gas bills—are these not ideal conditions for someone wanting to concentrate on his work? There was even a well-stocked library at my disposal, because, since 1989, the St. Louis penitentiary has been under the progressive directorship of the internationally renowned law professor, Jacob J. Seiberling. I had several occasions to speak to Dr. Jay-Jay, as he was known among inmates, about what he termed my "tragic" relationship with Walt Disney.

*

Martha met me on the day of my release. She appeared pleased to see me again. Jonathan, our firstborn, had recently settled down. He was renting a small bungalow not far from St. Louis, just across the Mississippi. He had become a father, and was living with Lucy, his girlfriend, and their three-year-old son, in Springfield, Illinois, the burial place of Abraham Lincoln. Their boy had been given the name Walter, strangely enough. We decided to visit Jon—Springfield is roughly halfway between St. Louis and Chicago. The drive (Martha had reclaimed my car in Marceline a few days before) took only a few hours. It was the first time I had seen my son in several years. We stayed at a hotel on Packer Road, across from the Air and Military Museum. There I shared a bed with my ex-wife for the first time in twenty years.

We met Jonathan and his little family for Sunday brunch. The Atchison, Topeka & Santa Fe Railway Line ran just behind their little house. Every half hour, we could hear a freight or passenger train clatter past. My son appeared untroubled to be seeing me again. Neither he nor his partner mentioned my stay in prison.

Lucy accorded me a degree of respect I'm not used to. Her near-reverential awe of me both pleased and slightly confused me. Ever since Jonathan had told me his girlfriend's name for the first time, I couldn't help thinking of the owl-girl in Williamsburg, Virginia. In my imagination, the lost girl who vanished on Halloween night in 1966, whom Hazel had told me about so vividly, was one and the same as the young woman, who, years later, became the mother of my first grandson. When we now met for the first time, therefore, I soon started to ask her questions about her childhood. Jonathan interrupted me: his girlfriend, who was half a year younger than himself, was perfectly willing to talk about all kinds of subjects, except her early years. That they regarded as Lucy's personal secret. So I confined myself to the jocular remark that my son and his partner might have met one another at a park for mobile homes.

"No, Dad," replied Jonathan, mildly scandalized. "Not at a parking site, but in Stella, Ohio, a little town exclusively created for mobile home owners. That's where I saw my Lucy for the first time. And I followed her to Tropic Farm, a similar sort of place in Southern Indiana. That's where we finally got acquainted."

They giggled like a pair of teenagers.

"Were you ever the owner of an owl costume, Lucy?" I made one final attempt.

She looked at me expressionlessly with her pale blue eyes. "I'm sorry, Dad, I don't understand the question." She remained friendly and affectionate, and served us a mild Calvados bottled in the town of Bayeux. She certainly wasn't aware that Bayeux is probably not more than twenty miles from Isigny-sur-Mer. And I didn't tell her, either.

My grandson remained asleep until early afternoon. When he awoke, he beamed at me, played with me, called me Bill, even though I usually go by William. "Bill, catch the ping-pong ball! Bill, tell me a story! Bill, I want a ride on your shoulders!"

At four o'clock, Jonathan turned down the lights in the living room and drew the curtains. He had thought of a surprise for us, he said. He switched on the television and the video machine, and put in a cassette. A short trailer followed for *The Lion King* and *Pocahontas*, two new masterpieces from the Walt Disney Studios, now available on video cassette. And then I heard the first few bars of a composition that has accompanied me for over forty years now, like a heart-beat, da-da-da-dahh-da-da, da-da-da-dahh-da-da! and so on, the tune called "Once Upon a Dream," the Tchaikovsky-inspired title music for *Sleeping Beauty*.

Walter became very quiet.

And we four grown-ups sat mesmerized for seventy-five minutes before the Technirama colors on the small screen. What a wonderful film! *My* film!

"Again!" shouted my grandson, as the words "The End" came up. "Bill! Again!"

Jonathan stood up, opened the curtains, swung his son up into the air, shook him and tickled him until my grandson was squealing with delight. "It's hard to imagine," his father whispered, "a world without Walt!"